Matchmaker, matchmaker, make Ellen a match. . . .

Jessica watched as Curtis bopped down the hall.

"This is not good," Lila said, clicking her tongue against the back of her throat.

"What are you talking about?" Jessica asked. "It's great. He's a guy. And he likes her. If Ellen's got a guy of her own, we're off the hook."

"Jessica." Lila sighed. "We're Unicorns. What one of us does reflects on the others. *Think.* Do we really want Ellen hanging out with that clown? I mean, did you catch that dumb surfer-dude accent? That act is like, so out. *Nobody* does surfer dude anymore."

"Lila's right," Kimberly said. "We've got to nip this in the bud."

Jessica had to admit, her friends had a point. Surfer dude was a social liability that the club couldn't afford. "But how?"

"By finding Ellen a guy who *is* right for her," Mandy said. "We'll split up. Search the ship from stem to stern. Find a guy who's worthy, and meet back at dinner with the day's catch. Is it a plan?"

"It's a plan," Jessica, Kimberly, and Lila agreed in unison.

Bantam Books in THE UNICORN CLUB series.
Ask your bookseller for the books you have missed.

#1 SAVE THE UNICORNS!
#2 MARIA'S MOVIE COMEBACK
#3 THE BEST FRIEND GAME
#4 LILA'S LITTLE SISTER
#5 UNICORNS IN LOVE
#6 THE UNICORNS AT WAR
#7 TOO CLOSE FOR COMFORT
#8 KIMBERLY RIDES AGAIN
#9 ELLEN'S FAMILY SECRET
#10 MANDY IN THE MIDDLE
#11 ANGELS KEEP OUT
#12 FIVE GIRLS AND A BABY
#13 WHO WILL BE MISS UNICORN?
#14 LILA ON THE LOOSE
#15 TOO COOL FOR THE UNICORNS
#16 BON VOYAGE, UNICORNS!

THE UNICORN CLUB®

BON VOYAGE, UNICORNS!

Written by
Alice Nicole Johansson

Created by
FRANCINE PASCAL

BANTAM BOOKS
NEW YORK•TORONTO•LONDON•SYDNEY•AUCKLAND

To Anna-Lily Chase

RL 4, 008-012

BON VOYAGE, UNICORNS!
A Bantam Book / February 1997

Sweet Valley High® and The Unicorn Club®
are registered trademarks of Francine Pascal.

Conceived by Francine Pascal.

Produced by Daniel Weiss Associates, Inc.
33 West 17th Street
New York, NY 10011.

Cover art by Bruce Emmett.

ISBN: 0-553-48444-3
Published simultaneously in the United States and Canada

Bantam Books are published by Bantam Books, a division of Bantam
Doubleday Dell Publishing Group, Inc. Its trademark, consisting of the
words "Bantam Books" and the portrayal of a rooster, is Registered in U.S.
Patent and Trademark Office and in other countries. Marca Registrada.
Bantam Books, 1540 Broadway, New York, New York 10036.

PRINTED IN THE UNITED STATES OF AMERICA

OPM   0 9 8 7 6 5 4 3 2 1

One

"Is that awesome or *what?*" Jessica Wakefield's blue-green eyes flickered over the enormous white cruise ship. She and her friends, Lila Fowler, Mandy Miller, Kimberly Haver, and Ellen Riteman stood on the dock along with hundreds of other excited seventh- and eighth-graders, waiting to board.

The sky was a clear blue, the sun was directly overhead, and the salty ocean breeze was cool. It lifted the tendrils of Jessica's honey blond hair off her shoulders and tickled her throat and ears.

"Awesome doesn't even begin to cover it." Mandy Miller shoved her big suitcase forward with her foot and shifted her fifties-style train case from one hand to the other.

Kimberly Haver and Ellen Riteman gazed at the *Caribbean Queen* in openmouthed admiration.

Jessica noticed that even her best friend, Lila Fowler, whose father was the richest man in Sweet Valley, California, and who had been on *three* cruises already, looked flushed with excitement.

"How does this compare with the cruise you took last year?" Mandy asked Lila.

"Five hundred times better," Lila responded with a broad grin. "Because *that* cruise was mostly people my dad's age. *This* cruise is all people our own age."

Jessica, Mandy, Ellen, and Lila were all seventh-graders at Sweet Valley Middle School in Sweet Valley. Kimberly Haver was an eighth-grader. The girls were all members of the Unicorn Club.

Jessica's heart fluttered with excitement. She'd never seen as many kids gathered in one place as were gathered on the dock. Most important—she'd never seen as many guys.

Hundreds of them.

Blond. Brunette. Tall. Short. Lean and lanky. Stocky and muscular. All of them cute. Really cute.

Yep! This cruise was going to be megaspectacular. Superfantastic. Hyperwonderful.

TEN DAYS OF SUN AND FUN FOR GRADES SEVEN AND EIGHT, the brochure had said. The trip was sponsored by *Dream Teen* magazine. Jessica was a subscriber. She had received the brochure a month ago and the Unicorns had immediately decided that they *had* to go.

Now here they were.

All it had taken was a month of nonstop extra chores, good behavior, A's (or at least B's) in school, made beds, and a truce on any and all forms of sibling rivalry. At least for Jessica, Kimberly, Mandy, and Ellen.

Lila was an only child. A very lucky only child. *In my next life, I want to come back as Lila,* Jessica thought as she watched Lila inch forward along the gangplank with her four pieces of matching Italian leather luggage, her totally hot, lime green ribbed-knit silk minidress, and her *très* expensive (gift from Daddy) French sunglasses.

The Unicorns' favorite sport was competing with each other, and Lila and Jessica were especially competitive. But today Jessica had to admit she was psyched that Lila and the others had gone all out on their wardrobes. After all, that made *her* look good.

Mandy had roamed the thrift shops and assembled the coolest retro resort wear wardrobe Jessica had ever seen. Double-knit shorts and tanks left over from the sixties. Two-piece bathing suits with boy-cut legs made out of that weird, heavy-duty girdle kind of material. Sandals and a bathing cap covered with sixties-style daisies. Mandy was Beach Blanket Bingo with attitude.

Jessica had decided to go simple. White shorts and lots of little tees with matching socks and deck shoes. And some short flippy skirts. With her California girl good looks, she decided to cultivate a "gorgeous without trying" look. It had only taken ten days of nonstop shopping to achieve.

Kimberly was athletic and wanted the hippest sportswear. She'd dragged Jessica with her to Weight Classy and bought out everything on the sale rack. Spandex. Spandex. Spandex. Kimberly was tall and muscular, so she really pulled off the look.

Ellen was the one Unicorn who hadn't made a special shopping trip for the cruise. Instead, she had just thrown some things in a bag—mostly just simple shorts and T-shirts. Even though she was the president of the club, she didn't get much into the competitive spirit.

Jessica had talked to the other girls about whether or not to say something to Ellen about her boring cruise wardrobe, but Mandy had convinced them all not to. Ellen's parents had gotten a divorce recently, and Ellen was still pretty bummed about it.

Besides, Mandy had pointed out, divorce was not only painful, it was also expensive—which probably meant Ellen had even less money for clothes than usual. There was no point in bugging her about a problem she couldn't do anything about.

Jessica had dropped the subject, but she wasn't convinced that money was the real problem. After all, Mandy didn't have much money and always managed to look great. Nope, Jessica was pretty sure the problem was in Ellen's attitude, not in her wallet.

But hey! Jessica couldn't spend her whole life worrying about Ellen. If the others were willing to let Ellen slack a little, Jessica could live with it.

The Unicorns were at the top of the gangplank now and filing past the Welcome desk. A very sophisticated looking high-school girl sat behind the desk wearing a blue-and-white nautical one-piece bathing suit and a yachting cap. She gave the girls a dazzling smile. "Welcome aboard," she said in a friendly voice. "May I have your names, please?"

"Jessica Wakefield, Lila Fowler, Kimberly Haver, Mandy Miller, and Ellen Riteman," Jessica answered.

"You're all together?"

"That's right," Kimberly said.

"All for one and one for all," Ellen added.

The hostess checked her passenger list and tapped it with her pencil. "Here you are. Two rooms across the hall from each other. Rooms 507 and 508." She pointed toward an enclosed area. "Up that stairway. Two flights. Just leave your suitcases, and a steward will bring them to your cabins." She gave the girls a mock salute. "Check out your cabins and then report to the main dining room on the second deck for our getting-to-know-you mixer. Snacks, sodas, and music. See you there."

She waved as the girls moved on so that the group behind them could check in.

"Only two rooms," Lila said in a worried tone as they shoved their big suitcases out of the way. "That means three people will have to share one room and two people will have to share the other."

"So?" Jessica shouldered her carry-on bag, which contained her makeup, toothbrush, hair spray, and bathing suit. She had a feeling it might take a while to get their bags delivered. No way was she going to take a chance of having to go to the first mixer without her natural-look makeup.

"So how are we going to decide who's in the cabin with three people and who's in the cabin with two?" Lila pressed.

"Here we go again." Kimberly rolled her eyes at Jessica.

"I've seen this movie before." Jessica laughed. "And it always comes out the same."

Not long ago the Unicorns had gone on a trip to a dude ranch. They'd gotten into a pretty heated argument about who had to room with whom.

"We'll draw straws," Mandy said stubbornly. "That's the only fair way."

"But I have a lot of clothes with me," Lila protested. "I don't think I can share a closet with *two* other people."

"We all have clothes, Lila," Mandy reminded her.

Lila flipped her glossy hair off her shoulders. "Not like mine."

Jessica gritted her teeth. Lila's bragging was starting to wear on her nerves, but she decided not to tell her off. Lila happened to have a little red silk slip dress that Jessica was hoping to borrow at least once on this trip. Starting a big fight with Lila would *not* be a good policy move. Not if she wanted to borrow that dress. "So how do you want to handle it?" she asked as cheerfully as she could.

"Well," Lila said. "I thought maybe I could share a cabin with Ellen. She doesn't have many clothes. That way, I'll have plenty of room to hang up everything I brought and it won't be wrinkled. And if anybody needs to borrow anything, it'll be right there and ready to go."

Jessica raised her eyebrow. Now she understood why Lila had treated them all to the big fashion show yesterday. Mandy had had a fit over the bell-bottom sailor suit with the midi blouse. Kimberly had gone gaga over a couple of Lila's Olympic-cut suits. And Jessica had made it clear that the red dress was a garment worthy of worship.

Lila had planned her whole strategy out in advance. In exchange for borrowing privileges, she'd get the most closet space.

"I think the three of us can be comfortable sharing, don't you?" Jessica said to Mandy and Kimberly.

"Absolutely," Mandy said quickly.

"No problem," Kimberly echoed.

"Ellen?" Jessica prompted.

"Hmm? Yeah, I guess." Ellen shrugged, as if it were all the same to her.

"Check it out! How totally cool! It's just like in the movies."

Lila watched Ellen press her face against the little round porthole that faced out to sea. Then she darted into the bathroom to inspect it. "Wow! Look at this. It's got like *everything*. Even a place to plug in an electric toothbrush."

Lila looked around, feeling almost as pleased as Ellen. The cabin wasn't as plush as she was used to—but then she was used to traveling with her father, and that meant first class all the way.

But the cabin was nice enough. Two beds with thick coverlets in a crisp white-and-blue check. The walls were covered with an off-white linen fabric with brass holes around the door frames, creating a sailing motif.

There was a knock at the door. Before Lila could say "Come in," two efficient stewards brought in their suitcases and disappeared back into the hallway, pushing an enormous dolly piled high with luggage.

"Who's here?" Ellen came out of the bathroom with an expectant smile on her face.

"The bags," Lila answered.

Ellen's face fell a fraction. "Oh. I thought maybe it was the others."

"They're probably unpacking," Lila said. "Chill out. They'll be here." *One, two, three, four, five.* Lila quickly counted the suitcases that had been delivered.

Great. Everything present and accounted for. Lila pulled the little gold key from her pocket to unlock them. "This is great. Really nice. We're lucky it's just the two of us. Think how crowded it would be if there were three of us in here."

"I wouldn't mind," Ellen said. "The more the merrier. I'm looking forward to some quality time with you guys. It feels like ages since the five of us have hung out together."

"No doubt," Lila agreed. "It's amazing how much social life I had to give up to do *all* my home-work. I had no idea."

"Try doing all your homework *and* baby-sitting *and* shuttling back and forth between two parents."

Lila watched as Ellen stuffed her underwear and makeup into the top drawer of the one dresser in the room.

"Oh, Ellen," Lila said quickly. "If you wouldn't mind . . . it's so much more convenient for me to have the top drawer. Would you mind taking the bottom drawer?"

"Sure. No problem." Ellen removed her things and began arranging them in the bottom drawer.

Lila went to the mirror and inspected her face, feeling very happy with the way she'd finessed the rooming situation.

Jessica would have argued with her over the top drawer thing. So would Kimberly. Mandy wouldn't have argued, but she would have made Lila feel childish and selfish for asking and Lila would have wound up letting her have the top drawer.

Ellen was going to be a great roommate. She

might be the president of the Unicorns, but she never tried to boss Lila or anybody else. And she was so eager for everybody to get along and be friends, she would agree to anything.

Lila pushed Ellen's few garments into a tight bunch at the very end of the closet and began hanging up her expensive new resort clothes.

"Look! Everybody's almost on the boat." Ellen leaned over the rail and pointed downward. The line on the gangplank was down to about thirty people.

The girls had finished unpacking and now stood on the outside deck of their floor, watching the scene below. The gangplank was still flush with the dock. The blue ocean lapped against its wooden piles and the sides of the ship.

Guys and girls chattered and laughed as they hurried up and down the decks and stairwells, exploring. But in spite of all the movement and excitement, the calm sea and still breeze made the day seem peaceful and quiet.

Ellen felt a distant pounding through the bottoms of her sandals. "Is that the engine?" she asked. "Are we leaving already? What about those people on the dock?"

Kimberly laughed. "Hel*lo*. That's music, Ellen. The mixer must be starting."

Ellen grinned. "Oh yeah. . . . Let's go party!"

She pumped her fist and followed Jessica,

Mandy, Kimberly, and Lila up the stairs to the deck where the dining room was located. The dining room was enclosed with windows that were opened to create a cross breeze.

Long tables held tray after tray of little sandwiches, fruit, and sodas. Ellen's mouth began to water. "Come on," she said. "Let's go check out the food. I'm starving."

Ellen headed toward the refreshment table, moving her head to the beat of the music. "This is going to be so cool. I mean, there are so many things we can all do together. Swimming. Bowling. Dance classes."

Ellen picked up a sandwich and took a bite. "Ugh. Salmon. Here Lila. You like salmon. Wanna finish this for me?" She turned to hand it to Lila— but no one was behind her.

Ellen looked around in confusion. Where was Lila? And Jessica? Where were Kimberly and Mandy? She didn't see them anywhere. Apparently, she'd been carrying on a conversation all by herself.

She wrapped the remainder of the sandwich in a napkin and looked around for a trash can. There wasn't one. The table was too pretty to just dump a dirty napkin, so she stuffed it in the pocket of her jeans. Then she pushed through the crowd to find her friends.

All around her, guys and girls chatted and laughed. Everybody looked completely at ease. Like they all knew each other or something. Ellen couldn't help feeling awkward.

Over the heads of some girls, she saw the top of Jessica's blond head. "Excuse me. Excuse me." Ellen pushed past a knot of guys until she located the Unicorns.

She could see them on the other side of the dining room talking with a bunch of guys. Really cute guys. And the next thing Ellen knew, the whole group was leaving through the door on the opposite side of the dining room.

Nobody even looked back to see where she was.

Ellen felt her heart sinking down into her stomach. She couldn't believe what an idiot she was. She'd pictured the Unicorns hanging out together as a club, but all her friends seemed to care about was meeting guys.

Ellen caught a glimpse of her reflection in the chrome frame of the window. She wasn't bad-looking or anything, but she wasn't the kind of girl guys went for.

The reflection in the chrome frame was as clear as the picture in a crystal ball. Ellen had a sharp and vivid glimpse of what the next ten days were going to be like. Hanging out all by herself while her friends hung out with guys.

Ellen clenched her fists. No way was she going to stand for that. If she got off the boat now, she could probably get some kind of refund. *And it wasn't like anybody would mind,* she reasoned.

Lila would probably be thrilled.

She could have the *whole* closet.

Two

"That's the bowling alley," a guy with brown hair and big hoop earrings told Mandy. He pointed toward a set of double doors with little round windows. "And on the deck right below it is the disco."

Mandy stood on her tiptoes and peered into one of the windows. Amazing. Six rows of alleys complete with bowling pins and everything. The ship had every kind of entertainment she could imagine.

"Let's go see the snack bar," a tall guy in a Dodgers baseball cap suggested. "Then let's go see what kind of equipment they have at the sports center. Somebody told me they even have a batting cage."

"Let's go downstairs first," a girl in a pair of khaki shorts suggested. "I want to see the shopping arcade."

The Unicorns were exploring the ship with nearly twenty other people—guys and girls who were eagerly checking out all the ship had to offer.

Mandy hurried down the stairwell behind Jessica; a short, muscular African American guy from San Diego; and the guy in the baseball cap. Behind her, she could hear Kimberly giggling with Lila.

"Wow!" Kimberly exclaimed when they reached the bottom of the stairs and entered the arcade. "It's like a mall. A floating mall."

Mandy couldn't wait to come back on her own and visit the art gallery and the craft shops. The stuff in the windows was amazing.

Mandy lingered in front of the hair salon, looking at the hair ornaments. She thought they were beautiful and totally imaginative, especially the ones made out of elongated mother-of-pearl–shaped shells. She remembered going shell hunting with Ellen after the last tropical storm. That was always the best time to find shells because they washed up on the beach. They'd collected a bunch of unbroken mother-of-pearl. Maybe she could make some ornaments that looked like the ones in the window for herself and Ellen.

"Look, Ellen." Mandy turned to see if Ellen had noticed the mother-of-pearl hair clips. Her eyes scanned the group that had strung out along the windows of the shopping arcade. Ellen was nowhere to be seen. "Hey, Jessica! Where's Ellen?"

Jessica tore her attention from a minidress hanging in a shop window. "Ellen? I don't know." She looked around, puzzled. "I thought she was with us."

Kimberly and Lila splintered away from the group. "Did we lose her?" Lila asked.

Mandy closed her eyes, trying to picture the last place she had seen Ellen. They had been in the dining room and Ellen had said something about checking out the food. "I don't think we lost her," Mandy said with a groan. "I think we forgot her in the dining room. Who wants to volunteer to go back?"

Jessica looked at Lila, who looked at Kimberly, who looked back at Jessica.

"*Guys*," Mandy pleaded.

"Ellen needs to learn to keep up with the group," Kimberly said impatiently. "We can't be running around looking for her all the time."

"Come on," Mandy urged. "All for one and one for all. Remember?"

"Yeah. But there's a limit," Lila remarked.

Mandy grabbed Lila's wrist. "Quit complaining and let's go," she commanded, pulling her friend along toward the dining room.

"OK, OK," Lila protested. "You don't have to pull my arm out of the socket."

"We'll be back," Jessica shouted over her shoulder to the group of sightseers.

By the time they reached the dining room, most of the other passengers had disbursed. A few kids stood chatting by the refreshment table, but Ellen wasn't one of them.

"Maybe she went back to the cabin," Kimberly suggested. "Let's go check."

Mandy led the group out on the main deck, and then jumped in surprise when a large air horn directly overhead blew a long and loud signal. She covered ears with her hands until it was over.

"*What* was that?" Jessica asked.

"The ship is about to sail," Lila explained. "Feel the engine?"

Mandy did feel a rumbling beneath her feet. And it wasn't the faint pounding of a bass guitar.

The girls hurried to the rail and leaned over to watch the ship pull away from the dock. The deck below them protruded out several feet. Mandy squinted—then let out a sharp cry.

Standing at the rail of the deck below was Ellen.

"What is she doing down there?" Kimberly demanded in an exasperated voice. "And why does she have her suitcase?"

"She's leaving the ship!" Jessica exclaimed with alarm. "Ellen!" she shouted.

But Jessica's voice was no match for the engines.

The gangplank, which had been flush with the dock, began to retract, leaving a space of about three feet between the edge of the main deck and the dock.

Ellen loped uncertainly back and forth along the edge of the deck as it moved slowly away from the dock. Then she appeared to reach a decision. She hoisted her suitcase over the rail and set it down.

Before Mandy could find her voice, Ellen had swung one long leg over the rail.

The ground below Mandy's feet shook as the engines shifted into gear. The space between the dock and the ship widened.

Ellen teetered on the edge for a second before bending her knees as if preparing for the high jump. Her hand gripped her bag.

"Ellen! Nooooo!" Mandy shrieked.

Ellen catapulted off the edge of the deck. Below her, the reflected sun twinkled and glittered on the blue surface of the water. Above her, the blue sky and white billowy clouds made her appear like a cutout figure in a collage.

Ellen hung there, suspended for a brief moment, her feet poised above the edge of the dock. Then, as if in slow motion, she began her downward descent.

Down. Down. Down and . . .

Jessica covered her ears, but she couldn't block out the sound.

Splash!

She heard Mandy and Lila groan.

Kimberly whistled. "She missed it by a centimeter!"

A split second later, horns and sirens pierced the air. Several pairs of footsteps clattered across the deck and down the metal stairwells. Jessica opened her eyes and saw what seemed like dozens of white uniformed men and women running in all directions.

"Passenger overboard!" echoed through the air over the engines and the surf.

Down in the water, Ellen dog-paddled in the direction of the dock with her suitcase bobbing behind her.

Splat!

A white tube smacked the surface inches away from her. She ignored the lifesaving device and continued toward the dock.

Splash!

Splash!

Two shirtless crew members dived over the side and stroked toward Ellen, reaching her within seconds.

One of them put his hand on her arm and the other grabbed her suitcase.

They were determined to save her.

There was only one problem.

Ellen didn't want to be saved.

"Let me go!" she shouted angrily, yanking at her backpack.

The surprised sailor lost his grip and Ellen swung the suitcase in a 180 degree circle, whacking the other sailor on the shoulder.

Ellen, the sailor, and the suitcase disappeared for a moment under the surface, before bobbing back up with Ellen flailing her arms and coughing up water.

The second sailor managed to grab her under the arms and began towing her back toward the ship.

Jessica looked from side to side. Then she looked up and down.

She didn't know where they had come from, but it seemed like every single kid on the cruise was assembled on the decks, watching the scene from over the rails. Several were laughing.

"This is not good," Kimberly murmured.

"Trust Ellen to do something to make us all look stupid," Lila muttered.

"What *was* she thinking?" Jessica wondered.

"I think we'd better find out," Mandy said. "Come on. They'll probably take her to the infirmary."

"There now," the ship's nurse said in a soothing voice. "More comfortable now?"

"I'm fine," Ellen replied. "Could you please see what you can do about booking me a helicopter? I really want to get off this ship."

The nurse chuckled and stuck a thermometer in Ellen's mouth.

Ellen rolled her eyes. Taking somebody's temperature must be in the nurse's union rules or something. She wasn't *sick*. She was just *wet*.

But she felt like somebody being prepped for open-heart surgery. The color scheme in the infirmary was white, white, white, and white with a chrome bedpan for color. Her wet clothes had been taken away to be laundered, and she was wearing one of those stupid paper gowns open down the back.

The bed was pretty comfortable. And if she hadn't felt so miserable and embarrassed, she might have gotten a kick out of elevating various parts of her body with the remote control.

"You don't want to get off the ship," the nurse soothed while Ellen held the thermometer under her tongue. "Why, you're as safe on a ship than you are in your own room in California. *Safer* if you live over a fault line." The nurse guffawed at her own joke.

Ellen removed the thermometer. "I'm not scared."

"It's nothing to be ashamed of," the nurse insisted, thrusting the thermometer back in Ellen's mouth. "Lots of people get nervous their first time out. You'll get used to it in no time."

The nurse disappeared around the curtain that separated Ellen's bed from the rest of the infirmary area. "I'll be back in a few moments with some tea."

Ellen flopped against the pillows. It was no use. She was talking to a wall wearing a white polyester dress with "Nurse Jenkins" embroidered over the pocket. She'd just have to wait until the ship docked at an island with an airport and then make her escape.

"Excuse me. We're friends of Ellen Riteman's. May we see her, please?"

Ellen froze. She recognized Mandy's voice on the other side of the curtain.

"Of course. Just step right around the curtain," the nurse answered.

Ellen yanked the thermometer from her mouth, turned over, pulled the covers up to her chin and closed her eyes, pretending to be asleep.

Nobody said a word, but Ellen could *feel* them tiptoeing around the curtain and gathering around her bedside.

She could *feel* Kimberly roll her eyes.

She could *feel* Lila scowl.

She could *feel* Jessica smother a giggle.

She could *feel* Mandy's fingernail scrape the bottom of her foot sending crawly, tickly, screamy feelings up her leg and straight to her brain where the audio system was connected. *"Yeooowww!"* Ellen screeched, opening her eyes and pulling her foot under the covers. "What are you doing?"

Mandy smiled. "I saw that on a hospital show. It's how they tell if people are alive or dead."

"I'm alive." Ellen sat up and arranged her covers with as much dignity as she could muster.

Jessica plopped down on the foot of her bed. "So what's with the big swan dive?"

Ellen took a deep breath. "I changed my mind about going on the cruise, that's all."

"But why?" Lila raised her shoulders practically up to her ears. "I don't get it. We worked so hard to get to go on this trip. Why were you trying to bail?"

"Because I realized it wasn't going to be the kind of trip I imagined," Ellen answered, a lump rising in her throat. "I thought we'd be spending time together. As a group. You know? But then, like, you all go off with a bunch of guys and leave me standing there like an idiot before the ship's even left the dock."

"We're sorry," Mandy said immediately. "We just didn't notice you weren't with us."

"Exactly my point!" Ellen cried.

Lila crossed her arms. "What do you expect us to do? Just hang out with girls? We could have stayed home and done that."

Ellen moved her feet down to the bottom of the bed, forcing Jessica to stand up. "Look. Don't worry about it. Just go on and do whatever you want. I'm going to take a nap."

She turned over and closed her eyes.

Mandy said softly. "We'll see you later."

Funny, she reflected as she heard them leave. She'd always thought she was really lucky to be in a club with the most popular girls in school.

Not anymore.

Maybe if her friends were a little less in demand, they'd have time for each other—and for her.

Three

Kimberly crossed her arms and tapped her foot. "Prognosis?"

Mandy shook her head. "Not good." She shot a glance at Jessica. "Suggestions?"

Jessica crossed *her* arms and leaned against the wall.

They were standing in the hallway outside the infirmary, plotting their strategy. "She feels left out."

"Right." Mandy nodded.

"So what we have to do is make sure she doesn't feel left out," Jessica said.

"How?" Kimberly demanded. "We don't want to hang out like a girl pack for this whole cruise just to make Ellen feel good. I want to meet some guys. We all do. Ellen's just going to have to get with the program."

"Let's face it. None of us is going to have any trouble meeting guys. But Ellen . . . " Lila shook her head, her voice trailing off.

"It's her own fault," Kimberly said briskly. "She's pretty. She's funny. But she just won't try. Look at those clothes she brought with her. They make no statement. No statement whatsoever."

"Correction," Lila said. "They do make a statement. They state 'I'm Ellen Riteman and I have no self-confidence, which is why I want to follow my four best friends around during the most romantic ten-day cruise of their lives.' "

"Let's not be so harsh," Mandy pleaded.

Jessica had to agree that Mandy had a point. Sometimes the Unicorns got a little carried away when they ragged on Ellen. They were supposed to be her friends. They should be looking for ways to help her, right? "Maybe we should try to find her a guy," Jessica mused.

"I don't think the ship offers a dating service." Kimberly giggled.

Lila laughed.

Mandy nudged her, pointing to the infirmary door.

"I'm serious," Jessica said. The more she thought about it, the more she liked the idea. "We should try to find somebody that Ellen would like and who would like her, and introduce them."

Lila rolled her eyes as if it were the dumbest idea she'd ever heard. "Who?"

"How?" Kimberly demanded.

"Where?" Mandy asked with a shrug.

"Exceeeuusee me, man," said someone behind Jessica. She recognized the accent immediately and cringed. Ughhhh. A surfer dude.

She turned and saw a guy with shoulder-length, white-blond hair, dark brows, long baggy shorts, and a floppy rayon Hawaiian shirt. He was skirting around the knot of girls, trying to get to the infirmary door. He clutched a small bunch of pink flowers that looked suspiciously like the centerpieces in the dining room.

He pushed the door open, giving them a lop-sided, apologetic smile. Then he did a kind of loose-limbed sidling step into the infirmary with his shoulders moving—as though he heard some kind of beat that nobody else could hear.

The door didn't swing all the way shut behind him, and Jessica could hear him talking to the nurse. "I'm looking for that really cool girl who jumped overboard."

Jessica widened her eyes. Had she just heard what she thought she heard? Who *was* this guy? And what did he want with Ellen?

She peered through the half-open door. She could feel Lila, Kimberly, and Mandy behind her, practically pushing her into the infirmary as they struggled to see what was going on over Jessica's head.

At the far end of the room, Ellen drew back the curtains and sat up in bed. "Me?"

The blond guy's head bobbled around on his neck. "Wow! Yeah. There you are. I brought yeeeuuuu some flowers. That dive, man? Totally parabolic."

"Parabolic?" Ellen repeated. She wasn't completely sure what that meant. And she wasn't sure if he was paying her a compliment or not.

"Here, man. These are for you." His long blond hair rippled as he thrust the flowers toward her, holding them out with a stiff, straight arm.

Ellen took the small bouquet and smiled. "Thanks," she said in a soft voice. "Thanks a lot." She felt a little warm flutter around her shoulder blades. This guy was cute.

"My name's Curtis," he said. "Curtis Bowman."

"I'm Ellen Riteman."

Curtis's head bobbed. "Cool."

Cool was a pretty ambiguous response, Ellen reflected. Was he saying he *liked* her name? Was he saying that it was OK with him if she wanted to call herself Ellen? Or was it merely another way of saying "check" or "gotcha"?

"Ellen?" The nurse came hurrying out of her cubicle carrying Ellen's clothes, freshly laundered. "You're dismissed as a patient. Captain Jackson would like to see you in his office." She handed Ellen her clothes. "Don't keep the captain waiting," she chirped.

Curtis's shoulders bobbed in the direction of the door. "I guess I'd better book and let you get dressed." He thrust his hand out. Ellen reached out tentatively, and he shook her hand vigorously. "So I'll see you around, Ellen." He gave her thumbs-up before sidling out the door.

As soon as he was gone, Ellen drew the curtain, snatched off the infirmary nightgown, and pulled on her jeans. She had to admit, Curtis Bowman was cute, and he was nice to give her the flowers. But so what? The way her luck went, he'd be interested in some other girl by dinnertime. She wasn't staying on this ship in the hopes that Curtis Bowman might work up some big crush on her. After all, what were the chances of that? She wasn't very smart or glamorous, and her favorite sport was whining. No, Curtis Bowman definitely wouldn't be interested in her for very long.

Her mind was made up. She wasn't staying on this ship. She'd tell Captain Jackson to see what he could do about evacuating her—ASAP.

When Jessica saw Curtis coming toward the door, she jumped backward, practically knocking her friends to the floor. The girls scrambled into place.

By the time Curtis walked out the infirmary door, the girls were standing exactly where they had been when he walked in.

He bobbed his head at Jessica and the others as he clumsily skirted around them again and then bopped down the hall.

"This is not good," Lila said, clicking her tongue against the back of her throat.

"Not good at all," Kimberly agreed.

Mandy just shook her head and sighed.

Jessica stared at the three grim faces. "What are you talking about? It's great. He's a guy. And he likes her. If Ellen's got a guy of her own, we're off the hook."

"Jessica." Lila sighed. "We're Unicorns. What one of us does reflects on the others. *Think.* Do we really want Ellen hanging out with that clown? I mean, did you catch that dumb surfer-dude accent? That act is like, so out. *Nobody* does surfer dude anymore."

"Lila's right," Kimberly said. "We've got to nip this in the bud."

Jessica had to admit, her friends were right. Surfer dude was a social liability that the club couldn't afford. "But how?"

"By finding Ellen a guy who *is* right for her," Mandy said. "We'll split up. Search the ship from stem to stern. Find a guy who's worthy, and meet back at dinner with the day's catch. Is it a plan?"

"It's a plan," Jessica, Kimberly, and Lila agreed in unison.

They lifted their hands and executed a quick and efficient four-way high five.

*   *   *

Lila hurried down the thickly carpeted hallway along which the better shops were located. She had been chafing to get off on her own and look around. Sometimes being the only rich girl in the crowd was a nuisance. Nobody else could afford to shop in her league, and it would have been nice to have somebody to trawl the expensive boutiques with.

A colorful window caught her eye. Fine jewels sparkled on a shelf piled high with white sand. A tropical print silk scarf had been draped artistically over a branch of driftwood as a backdrop.

Lila opened the heavy beveled glass door of the shop and went in. She might not find a guy for Ellen. But maybe an expensive present would make her feel better. It had been at least forty-eight hours since Lila had bought anything, and she was beginning to feel jittery.

Classical music played softly in the background, and the air was full of the scent of expensive perfume. Beautifully designed crystal bottles were displayed at a counter. Lila recognized several hard-to-find, foreign brands.

A saleswoman acknowledged her presence with a smile, but continued her conversation with a guy who looked not too much older than Lila.

"This is quite light," the saleslady said. "Many women prefer it to the heavier floral scents." She dabbed a bit on her wrist and held it out for him to smell.

"That's very nice," the guy said, breathing deeply. "I'll take the largest size you have."

Lila watched as he pulled a gold credit card from his wallet and handed it to the saleslady.

Maybe she'd come to the right place after all. She smiled. "That's my favorite perfume," she said.

The guy turned and Lila couldn't help admiring his square jaw and his thick black hair. "Really?" His lips smiled, but his eyes didn't.

Lila knew that smile. It was the *I have to be polite because that's how I was raised, but what could somebody like you possibly have in common with somebody like me?* smile.

Undeterred, Lila extended her hand. "I'm Lila. From Sweet Valley."

"I'm Jared Matthews. From San Francisco."

"The Bay Area?"

Jared nodded and bent over to sign the credit card slip that the saleslady had discreetly laid on the countertop. He scribbled his signature. The saleslady handed him his receipt and credit card, and he put them back in his wallet.

"Do you know the Hortmills?" Lila asked, watching him push the expensive leather wallet into his back pocket. Mr. Hortmill was a wealthy industrialist who had invested in several of Lila's father's ventures.

Jared's icy smile began to thaw. "Yes. They live down the street from me. Do you know them?"

"Oh yes," Lila said. "I met them in Switzerland."

"You ski?" Jared asked, interested now.

"Yes." Lila suddenly remembered her mission. "With my friend, Ellen. Ellen Riteman. Her family invited me to go along with them last Christmas."

Jared squinted. "Riteman. Riteman," he muttered, as if he were trying to place the name.

"The California Ritemans," Lila said, making it sound significant. "You've heard of them, of course." The inflection of her voice said, *if you haven't, you must be a total nobody.*

"I've heard of them. Sure." Jared smiled.

"Why don't you have dinner with us?" Lila suggested. "You can meet her."

Jared smiled. "Thank you. I'd love to."

"See you at dinner, then." Lila fluttered her fingers and hurried from the shop.

Lila smiled to herself with satisfaction. She had found a guy for Ellen and she'd found a winner.

Handsome.

Rich.

And a snob.

He's perfect, Lila thought.

Goin' on a manhunt, la da de da, la da de da.

The lyrics to the popular rock song echoed in Jessica's brain. She was standing on her tiptoes, peering into the window of the video arcade.

She was pleased to see that there were lots of guys in there. But how was she going to pick out the one who was right for Ellen?

The tall lanky guy with the red curls was cute. But he had tons of buddies standing around him. It would be too hard to strike up a conversation with him and work Ellen into it.

She noticed that there was a long line at the concession stand. Jessica grinned. Standing in line was always a good time to strike up a conversation.

Jessica bent over from the waist, swung her hair back and forth, and then threw her head back to get maximum hair volume. She whipped her Very Berry lipstick from the pocket of her shorts and touched up her lips.

Here goes, she thought. She stretched out her arm and sailed into the swinging door, giving it a hard push.

Blam!

"Ouch!"

Jessica jumped back when she heard the cry of pain from the other side of the door. A few seconds later, it swung slowly open and a pair of big brown eyes peered cautiously out. She couldn't see a nose or mouth, because the victim had his hand cupped over them.

"I think you were going in the 'out' door," he said in a muffled tone.

Jessica stared in horror. *Out* was written across the door she had just tried to enter in big red letters. "I am soooo sorry," she breathed. "Are you OK?"

The big brown eyes met hers and crinkled in a smile. "I think so. You tell me." He removed his hand and Jessica got the full view of one of the friendliest faces she had ever seen. "Well?" he prompted in an expectant tone. "Is it on straight?" He crossed his eyes, as if trying to examine his nose himself.

"It looks straight to me," Jessica replied, trying not to giggle. "I feel really terrible about this."

"Hey! It was an accident." He uncrossed his eyes. "A lucky accident. Because I made a new friend. At least I hope we'll be friends. I'm Sam. Sam Sloane."

"I'm Jessica Wakefield."

Sam's eyes lit up. "Jessica! Oh, wow! That's like, my very favorite name."

Jessica blushed. "Oh come on. You're just saying that."

"No. Really. I *love* that name. Where are you from?"

"Sweet Valley."

"That's in California."

"Uh-huh.

Sam shook his head and put his hands on his hips. "You are so lucky. I'm from Oregon, but California is my very favorite state. It's *beautiful. Gorgeous. Unbelievable.* And the girls . . . " Sam's mouth opened and closed, as if there just weren't enough superlatives in the dictionary to describe California girls.

Jessica stared at him. Was he putting her on?

"What can I say?" he finished. "They're just fabulous, that's all. So Jessica—*love* that name—are you here by yourself or with some friends or what?" His smile was so genuine and his eyes so full of interest, that Jessica's suspicions evaporated. He was for real.

"I'm with some friends. Four girlfriends," she added quickly, hoping to work Ellen into the conversation. "I'd love you to meet them. Why don't you sit with us at dinner?"

"*Fantastic!* Dinner with five California girls. Am I a lucky guy or what?"

Jessica grinned. She couldn't help it. Sam's enthusiasm was infectious. "Look for me in the dining room and I'll save you a seat."

He gave her the thumbs-up sign and a grin.

Jessica pivoted sharply so that her blond hair would fly out in a semicircle, as in a California girl shampoo commercial.

What a cutie, she thought as she hurried back toward her cabin. Sam was funny and ferociously enthusiastic about everything. Even things that weren't really that exciting. It was nice, but it also made her realize that Sam's standards weren't all that high.

Sam Sloane was the perfect guy, Jessica thought.

For Ellen, that is.

Four

"You're telling me you don't have a helicopter!" Ellen exclaimed in dismay.

Captain Jackson shook his head. "No helicopter," he confirmed. "Sorry."

"But I want to get off this ship. I want to go home. Today!"

Captain Jackson looked less than sympathetic. "I'm afraid that's not possible."

"But what if somebody had an emergency?" Ellen persisted. "You'd figure out some way to get them off the ship and back home? Wouldn't you? I mean, you'd *have* to. It's in the Geneva Convention or the Maritime Code of Conduct or something like that. You can't hold me hostage on this thing. It's cruel and unusual."

Captain Jackson's tight smile disappeared and

he drew himself up on the other side of his desk. Suddenly, his white uniform looked starchier and frighteningly official against his brown skin. He looked more like a navy admiral than the captain of a cruise ship.

He glowered and Ellen shrank down in her seat, feeling like a lowly swabby about to be court-martialed.

"Miss Riteman," he said, "a dispute among teenage girls does not qualify as an emergency—by any definition. We have no way of returning you home, so you will have to learn to get along with your companions or make a friend of solitude. Your ill-considered behavior created a great deal of disruption on my ship. If there are any more incidents like the one that took place this afternoon, I shall be forced to take disciplinary measures. Do I make myself clear?"

Ellen got a mental picture of herself in the brig, wearing big heavy chains on her ankles. *"Dear Mom: Don't worry about me. They tell me the penal colony is gorgeous this time of year."*

"Yes, sir," she said softly. "I understand."

Captain Jackson smiled. Sort of. It wasn't a real smile, Ellen knew. It was a forced smile. The kind of smile kids got from adults who really didn't like kids. "I'm here to help you," he said. "And if you have any problems, feel free to come to me. In the meantime, have fun. And that's an order," he barked.

"Yes, sir!" Ellen jumped up from her chair and backed toward the door.

On her way out, she noticed a framed certificate. "Admiral Matthew Jackson. U.S. Navy. Honorable Discharge." Below it, in the same frame, was a silver star. "For Heroism."

Ellen closed the door. That explained a lot. Captain Jackson was determined to lead his troops into a fun time—even if it killed them.

At six o'clock, Jessica hurried into the dining room and sat down at a large round table. Plenty of room for the Unicorns, Sam, and any other guys who might want to join a table full of gorgeous girls.

Dinner didn't really start until 6:15, so there weren't many people in the dining room yet. White-coated waiters were still setting up. They looked very busy and important as they checked the place settings, wiped spots off the glasses, and arranged the white-and-pink centerpieces.

Jessica smiled with pleasure. Everything was absolutely beautiful. And every time one of the waiters came in or out of the swinging doors that led to the kitchen, Jessica smelled something delicious.

Her mouth watered and her stomach rumbled. She was hungry. Once they got this Ellen thing worked out, she figured the rest of the cruise would be smooth sailing. She giggled at her own pun.

Lila walked in, and Jessica noticed she had changed out of her silk shorts and camp shirt into a blue-and-pewter paisley rayon dress with a shirred bodice and a drapey skirt that fell to her ankles. She sat down at the table, unfolded her napkin, and smirked. "I found him."

"Who?"

"Ellen's Mr. Right. His name is Jared Matthews."

Jessica frowned. "No way," she argued. "I found Ellen's Mr. Right and his name is Sam Sloane."

"Sam Sloane!" Lila repeated. "What a totally plebeian name."

"It's a great name," Jessica argued hotly. "And he's a great guy."

"I went to a lot of trouble to get Jared Matthews to sit with us and . . . " Lila broke off when Mandy and Kimberly came hurrying in together.

"I found a guy for Ellen," Mandy said breathlessly, taking a seat. "He's coming to dinner."

"Me too," Kimberly said.

Jessica sighed deeply. "We all found guys," she said. "So what are we going to do?"

"Just act natural," Mandy instructed. "Don't act like it's a setup or anything. I didn't tell Jack I wanted him to meet somebody. Did you guys?"

"Do I look like an idiot?" Kimberly asked angrily. "Of course I didn't tell Peter it was a setup. He probably wouldn't have agreed to sit with us."

Mandy pushed her hair behind her ears. "Jessica? Lila?"

Jessica shook her head. She hadn't said a word to Sam about Ellen—*yet*.

"I *mentioned* Ellen to Jared," Lila said. "That's all."

"Fine then," Mandy said with a smile. "Let's just let everybody get to know each other and . . ."

"And what?" Lila demanded angrily. "Let Jared Matthews get away? You're crazy."

Jessica snapped open her snowy white napkin and carefully arranged it on her lap. "Once you guys see Sam, you'll be ready to throw them all back," she promised. "Jared Matthews included."

"Shh," Mandy warned. "Here comes Ellen."

Jessica couldn't help feeling irritated. Ellen hadn't made any effort with her appearance at all. She'd just put on another pair of jeans and a T-shirt. Her chin-length hair was still wet from her escape attempt and it hung around her face in limp spirals that looked like overcooked noodles.

She took her seat. There was an awkward pause.

"Hi," Ellen said.

"Hi," Jessica said.

Ellen reached for a bread stick, took a bite, and chewed moodily. Jessica shot Mandy a *say something* look.

"So?" Mandy said. "Feeling any better?"

"Nope." Ellen took another bite of the bread stick. "And by the way, I had to go see the captain."

"Ohhhhh." Jessica giggled. "*Captain* sounds so romantic. What was it like?"

Ellen fixed her with a resentful glare. "Picture Mr. Clark in a white uniform, threatening you with the brig instead of detention."

"Oh." Jessica pressed her lips together. It was going to be harder than she thought to get Ellen's thoughts running along romantic channels.

She spotted Sam moving in her direction with a big smile on his face. She waved and gestured to the empty seat next to Ellen. "Sam. Sit down and meet Ellen, Lila, Mandy, and Kimberly."

Sam sat and grinned at each girl. Then he closed his eyes, as if trying hard to commit something to memory. He opened his eyes and pointed around the table. "Kimberly. Mandy. Lila. And Elaine. Am I right?"

Jessica's stomach sank. It wasn't like she'd expected love at first sight or anything like that, but she'd hoped he'd at *least* get Ellen's name straight.

An hour later, Ellen let out a sigh of relief when Lila and Jared got up to dance and Jessica and Sam went over to inspect the dessert buffet.

She was starting to get embarrassed, listening to Jessica and Lila talk about her to Jared and Sam. She felt like a backward kid with two ambitious mothers. *Ellen has such good taste. Ellen has so many friends. Ellen is such a joiner. Such a leader. Such a . . .* Ellen groaned. If it hadn't been so painful, their attempts to interest the two boys in Ellen would have been funny.

Thank goodness Mandy and Kimberly weren't trying to match her up.

On the other hand, maybe they were.

Two guys named Jack and Peter had come over to sit with Mandy and Kimberly. Fortunately, the four of them were sitting on the opposite side of the table and were too far away to talk to Ellen over the big band music.

Across the table, Mandy and Kimberly stood up. Mandy leaned over. "Ellen, Kimberly and I are going to get some air. Why don't you talk to Jack and Peter while we're gone?"

"But—" Ellen clamped her mouth shut. Mandy and Kimberly were already scurrying across the dining room.

Ellen looked warily at Jack and Peter. Jack fiddled with his napkin. Peter crumbled what was left of his poppy seed roll.

Ellen watched them, wondering which one would crack first.

It was Jack. He stood, said something to Peter, then leaned over the table. "It was nice to meet you," he shouted.

Ellen nodded. Yeah, right. A real thrill.

Jack hurried toward a knot of guys and girls talking to the DJ.

Ellen stared at Peter and smiled.

Peter smiled back.

Ellen kept staring.

Peter licked his lips and his eyes flickered nervously.

Ellen stared harder.

Peter stood up. "Nice to meet you," he shouted, then he hurried off, disappearing into the dance floor.

Chicken, Ellen thought.

"Look at that raspberry tart. I'll bet Ellen would *love* that," Jessica said. "In fact, let's get two. I'll bet she can eat them both."

Sam's eyes narrowed skeptically. "I don't know. Elaine didn't seem to have much of an appetite."

"Ellen," Jessica corrected. "Her name is Ellen."

"It is? Gosh, I wonder why she didn't say anything. I called her Elaine all through dinner."

I noticed, Jessica thought. Sam had tried to talk to Ellen—"Elaine"—two or three times, but Ellen had just grunted.

"Ellen is so easygoing," Jessica improvised. "She's just not the kind of girl who would get annoyed with a guy for getting her name wrong. She's too busy enjoying life to get bent out of shape by little things like that."

"Really?" Sam took a piece of key lime pie for himself. "I didn't get that impression. She doesn't seem too . . . ummm . . . *extroverted*."

"That's because she doesn't want to hog the spotlight," Jessica explained. "When Ellen gets going, she's the center of attention. She's the happiest most fun-loving girl in California."

Sam glanced back at the table where Ellen sat by herself, still picking at her food.

"Happy, happy, happy," Jessica said, wishing Ellen would *try* to look less like a basset hound.

"I think my father knows a Clint Riteman," Jared said thoughtfully. "Is that Ellen's father?"

Lila and Jared were dancing to one of the old, big band ballads that were being piped into the dining room during dinner. Jared had been polite to everyone during dinner. But it was pretty clear to Lila that he wasn't too impressed with most of the people at the table. He had had very little to say to anyone except Lila and Ellen.

And Ellen had been too glum to notice Jared's interest. She had barely responded to his attempts to make conversation. Lila had kicked her once under the table, trying to give her a hint. But Ellen responded by telling her to watch where she was putting her feet.

"I think she has an uncle named Clint," Lila lied. "I met him one summer when Ellen and her family took me to the Cayman Islands. He was getting incorporated or something."

Jared turned the corners of his mouth down as if he were impressed. "Yes. I understand the Caymans offer a lot of tax advantages to well-to-do people."

"Oh, the Ritemans are very well-to-do," Lila said quickly. "And very aristocratic."

She glanced over at Ellen, who was still poking at her dinner with her fork. She took a bite of something, chewed, then her face crumpled in disgust, and she spit whatever she was eating into her napkin.

Gross, Lila thought irritably.

She felt Jared stiffen.

"And very eccentric," Lila added as quickly as possible. "Her parents gave Ellen an experimental education. Like . . . ummm . . . they don't believe in table manners."

"Huh?"

"Yeah," Lila babbled on, improvising. "They decided that table manners are common. So they just all shovel their food in their mouths and spit it out if they don't like it."

"Unusual," Jared said.

"The Ritemans are unusual," Lila agreed. "But when you're that rich, you can be as unusual as you want."

I'd sell my soul for a bag of cheese and onion twists, Ellen thought, staring down at her untouched plate. The dinner had been fancy. So fancy she couldn't identify a thing on her plate. She'd taken a bite of what looked like a potato croquet, only to discover it was some kind of very fishy-tasting fish.

She dipped her fork in a puree of something and

tentatively licked one of the prongs. Gag! She choked and reached for her water.

At the next table, Curtis Bowman caught her eye and grinned. At least, she thought he was grinning at her. She glanced around to see if there was some other girl sitting behind her he might be flirting with. There wasn't. No, he was definitely grinning at her.

Ellen smiled tentatively back at him. That was all he needed. He came hurrying over, sitting down in the chair that Jared had occupied. "This food is gnarly," he said.

"Gnarly is an understatement," Ellen agreed. "Did you taste that grayish green stuff?"

"Yeah, man. What *is* that, anyway?" Curtis shuddered. "Know what would taste totally awesome right now? Some coconut puff dream creams and a big bag of barbecued corn chips."

Ellen's gastric juices began to flow at the very thought of it. "You like junk food?"

"I'm a junk food gourmet," Curtis answered.

The big band music ended and a blasting, heavy metal beat began to shake the room.

Curtis's bobbing head began bobbing from side to side rather than up and down. "Wanna dance?"

Dance? Ellen felt flattered but sort of horrified at the same time. It was nice of Curtis to ask, but she'd already made a fool of herself once today. "I think I'd better sit this cruise out," she answered with an uneasy laugh. "I don't really know how to dance."

"Me neither. So we'll be a good team."

He took Ellen's hand and led her to the dance floor. They stood face-to-face. Suddenly, Ellen felt really shy. And when her eyes met Curtis's, she blushed deeply.

Curtis studied the couple beside them, who moved their hips and shoulders in a sinuous way. Then he began to copy their moves in a comically exaggerated fashion.

Ellen giggled. Her shyness was beginning to disappear. She began to mirror Curtis's movements.

Curtis lifted his arm and moved his hand like a wave back and forth.

Ellen did the same.

He took her hand and instead of twirling her under his arm, he twirled himself under her arm.

Ellen could hear the people around them laughing.

Curtis made a silly face, thrusting his tongue down into his lower lip, and pointing to the ceiling. Ellen opened her mouth as wide as she could and jerked her elbow up like a chicken wing.

"Having fun?" Curtis shouted.

Much to Ellen's surprise, she was.

Jessica put the desserts on the table and looked around. Where was Ellen?

A burst of laughter drew her attention to the dance floor.

Uh-oh.

She looked wildly around trying to find Lila or Kimberly or Mandy.

She spotted Mandy, caught her attention, and jerked her head toward the dance floor. "Red Alert" she mouthed. "Do something!"

Mandy nodded her head. *I'm on it,* the nod said.

Mandy made a bee line back toward the ladies' room where Kimberly was chatting with some other girls.

Mandy grabbed Kimberly's arm, pulled her aside, and gestured toward the dance floor. When Kimberly saw Ellen and the surfer dude, her face turned grim. She and Mandy held a whispered conference and then started toward the dance floor.

"Isn't that Elaine?" Sam said.

"Ellen!" Jessica practically snapped. She grabbed Sam's arm, spun him around so that he faced away from the dance floor, and shoved him into a seat. "No, that's not her. Ellen's a really good dancer. A *great* dancer. A *fabulous* dancer. If you saw Ellen dance, you'd think you were watching a professional."

"Does Ellen always dance that way?" Jared asked.

Huh? Lila turned and almost choked. Ellen was out on the dance floor acting like a fool. Dancing with that surfer dude idiot and making stupid gestures with her hand and mouth. Opening her mouth and jerking her arm up every time the drum hit the downbeat—sort of like a chicken.

"Ummm . . . ummm . . . " She took Jared's arm and steered him toward the door. "There's something I should tell you."

She practically shoved him out of the dining room, determined to keep him from watching Ellen act like a fool.

Out on the deck, night was falling. A salty breeze fluttered over Lila's shoulders and lifted her hair.

It ruffled through Jared's thick curls. Lila thought his profile looked quite noble against the soft gray sky with its streaks of crimson.

"Ellen has the hereditary Royal Riteman family tic," she said. "That's one of her most aristocratic characteristics."

Jared raised his eyebrows. "A tic? You mean like, an involuntary motion?"

"Exactly!" Lila cried. "See, ummm, Ellen is a descendent of the Royal Family of . . . ummm . . . Sabolaslavichnia. And you know how those royal families were. They couldn't just marry *anybody*. So the same few noble families kept marrying and marrying each other, generation after generation. Now anybody who's *anybody* in Sabolaslavichnia has the Royal Riteman tic. You can't even get a restaurant reservation without it."

"Wow!" Jared breathed. "The Royal Riteman tic, huh?"

Lila nodded.

"You know. I knew she was special," Jared remarked thoughtfully. "I knew it the minute I saw her."

Ellen felt a tap on her shoulder and turned.

It was Mandy. "Mind if I cut in?" she asked.

Without waiting for an answer, Mandy inserted herself between Ellen and Curtis. A hand closed over Ellen's upper arm and the next thing she knew, Kimberly was pulling her off the dance floor toward the exit.

"Where are we going?" she asked.

"Back to the cabin to write some postcards," Kimberly said.

"But I don't want to write postcards."

"You said you wanted us all to spend some time together."

"Yeah! But not now," Ellen protested.

"Tough," Kimberly barked.

As they neared their cabin, Ellen heard several more sets of footsteps behind them. She turned and saw Mandy and Jessica following.

"Uh-oh. What is this?"

"A Unicorn meeting," Kimberly answered.

"That guy is such a phony," Jessica said.

"He's a total jerk," Mandy added.

"Geekoid!" Kimberly pronounced.

"He's not good enough for you," Lila said, sitting

down on the bed beside Ellen. They were all in the cabin she shared with Ellen, and it was pretty crowded. Lila wished Kimberly would get her feet off of her pillow, but she decided not to say anything. She could always call housekeeping to change her pillowcase. Right now it was more important to keep Ellen from ruining her life—or at least the cruise.

"But I like him," Ellen said. "At least I think I do. Or I might, if you guys would just let me talk to him."

"Ellen," Kimberly pleaded. "Think of the club. You're the president and you have a responsibility to set an example for the rest of us. If you start hanging out with some completely unsuitable guy, there's no telling what could happen. Now take this guy Peter. He's . . . "

"He's all wrong," Jessica finished for her. "Forget him."

"He's a great guy," Kimberly argued.

"No. Sam is a great guy. Peter is just some guy you found on the tennis court. We don't know anything about him."

"I know he's got a great serve," Kimberly said angrily. "Which is more than we can say about Mr. Geewhizgoshthat'sgreathowfabulous Sam Sloane."

Jessica jumped to her feet. "Don't you dare make fun of Sam."

"There's no point to this argument, because they're both wrong for Ellen," Mandy cried. "If any of you had taken the time to talk to Jack for just two minutes—"

Lila put her fingers to her lips and let out her shrillest whistle. She opened the door to the cabin. "It's getting late and I think Ellen and I need some sleep. So . . . "

Jessica sighed. "Let's get out of here." She got up, and the others followed. "We'll talk in the morning," Jessica said as they filed out.

Lila closed the door, locked it, and then whirled around. Ellen sat on the bed with her chin cupped in her hands, staring moodily at the wall. Lila danced over to her side, pulled her to her feet, and twirled her around. "Don't listen to them. Listen to Lila, your fairy godmother. The prince is interested."

"Huh?"

Lila opened the closet door, grabbed an expensive linen halter dress from the rack, and held it up in front of Ellen. "Jared Matthews is interested in you in a big way."

Ellen waved her hand. "Get out of town."

"No. I'm serious. He told me."

"Really?"

"Really" said Lila. "But he's not going to fall into your hands just like that. You're going to have to do a little work, Cinderella. Oh, and by the way, I don't know if you've ever heard of Sabolaslavichnia, but . . . "

Five

"Now remember. You're rich. You're sophisticated. You've seen it all and you've done it all. Nothing surprises you. Nothing impresses you. It's nice to be here, but it's no big deal. Now say it again," Lila commanded.

"Dahhhhhhling," Ellen drawled in a bored and languid voice, "isn't this all just toooooo cute." She walked across the cabin with an unhurried gait, her head swiveling slowly as she peered at imaginary scenery over the tops of Lila's expensive sunglasses.

"Better," Lila said. "But don't go overboard."

Ellen examined her reflection in the full-length mirror mounted on the back of their cabin door. Lila's coral-colored halter dress fit her perfectly. So did Lila's broad-brimmed straw hat with the coral chiffon scarf wrapped around the crown. Natural woven leather sandals made her legs look brown and smooth. But the tiny pearlized coral purse with its little girl handle made her want to gag. She looked like Shirley Temple. "It's too late. I'm already overboard. I look like an idiot."

Lila's eyebrows met over her nose. "You look like me. Are you saying *I* look like an idiot?"

"You can carry off an outfit like this. I just look like a paper doll or something."

"You look like one of the California Ritemans," Lila said tartly. "And don't forget it. Now come on. We don't have much time."

The boat had stopped at the island of St. Simone and would remain there until lunchtime. Passengers were free to disembark and sightsee.

Jared had called Lila and Ellen's room before breakfast and invited them to join him for a morning of sightseeing. Lila had accepted eagerly. She seemed to feel sure that romance was going to blossom between Ellen and Jared. Ellen wasn't so sure. She wasn't even sure she *wanted* it to blossom. Jared was so out of her league it was ridiculous.

But Lila had coached her for two hours. Ellen had to admit, Lila did really seem to care about her to go to all that trouble. The least Ellen could do was try.

They hurried up to the main deck where Jared stood waiting in long khaki shorts and a navy polo shirt. "Good morning, Ellen. Good morning, Lila. Ready to sightsee?"

"You bet," Ellen said eagerly. An elbow in her ribs left her breathless for a moment. "Even though I've seen it all before," she added in the politely bored voice Lila had taught her.

The three of them walked down the gangplank onto the docks of St. Simone. The area was crowded with vendors and street performers. A group of smiling young men pounded out a tune on some metal canisters. Ellen hurried in their direction. "Wow! What's that?"

"*Ellen!*" Lila stood beside her and stepped on her toe. "Stop trying to be funny. You know perfectly well those are steel drums. You've been in the Caribbean tons of times."

Ellen smiled like she imagined a rich eccentric might smile. In fact, she smiled so hard that her curled upper lip left a dab of sticky coral-colored frosted lipstick on the cartilage between her nostrils. "Ha ha ha ha ha."

"The Ritemans have *such* an offbeat sense of humor," Lila tittered, giving Ellen a dirty look.

Ellen noticed Jared looking at her with a slightly bewildered expression. She tried to think of something to say but came up empty. *Looks like it's time for a Royal Riteman tic attack,* she thought.

Ellen opened her mouth wide and jerked her elbow up. Her little bitty purse flew up along with it and . . .

Clang!

. . . bounced off the edge of one of the steel drums, creating a discordant note.

"Hey, mon, watch what you're doing," one of the musicians cautioned in his lilting Caribbean accent.

Ellen smiled serenely, as if she were completely unaware that she'd done anything unusual, then turned away, walking toward the shops. "Let's look at jewelry," she said.

Jared fell into step beside her and Ellen stared at her coral painted toes, wishing she could think of something sophisticated and rich to say. She couldn't, but she realized she was practically trotting along the street when she was supposed to be strolling. Ellen slowed, and swiveled her head from side to side, peering over her sunglasses. Left. Right. Left. Right. Left. Right. She began to feel slightly sick.

"So Ellen, which is your favorite island?"

"Oh . . . you know . . . ."

"Which ones have you visited?"

Ellen searched her mental map of the Caribbean, trying to think of some names. "Greenland," she said.

Jared raised an eyebrow. "I meant warm-weather islands."

Greenland's not warm? Ellen thought wildly. *Then how come they call it Greenland and not Iceland. Wait a second. There is an Iceland. But if Greenland's cold, then Iceland must be* . . . "Iceland," Ellen said decisively.

She knew from his face that she'd said something

dumb. She smiled, leaving a dab of lipstick on the bottom part of her nose and laughed. "Ha ha ha ha ha ha."

Jared smiled uncertainly. "You're a very unusual girl, Ellen."

Ellen wasn't sure if that was a compliment or not. *When in doubt, tic,* she decided. Ellen opened her mouth as wide as she could and jerked her elbow up. Her little bitty purse flew up and clipped Jared right in the jaw.

"Diamonds are nice, but soooooo common. I mean, *everybody* has diamonds, right? I much prefer an emerald." Ellen oozed up the gangplank next to Jared with her hips swiveling one way and her head swiveling the other.

Jessica leaned over the rail, watching her approach. *Why is she walking like that? She looks like an oscillating fan.*

"Helloooo Jessicaaaahhhh," Ellen drawled, fluttering her fingertips in Jessica's direction as she and Jared stepped onto the boat and walked arm and arm along the deck.

Lila, trailing about seven yards behind, gave Jessica a smug wink and paused beside her. "Well? Am I good or what?"

"What did you do to her?" Jessica stamped her foot in frustration. "She looks like an idiot."

Lila put her hands on her hips. "Oh, really.

Well, if you think my clothes make Ellen look like an idiot, then I'm sure you won't want to borrow any and run the risk of looking like an idiot yourself."

"Don't try to blackmail me," Jessica shot back. "I had a feeling something like this was going on when I couldn't find either one of you after breakfast."

"Something like what? What are you so upset about?"

"You've ruined everything, that's all. Sam will think she's a total weirdo."

Lila's head and chin jutted forward. "Read my lips, Jessica. I got her a guy. I thought that was the plan."

Jessica rested her elbows on the rail and her face in her hands. "Yeah, but that guy's all wrong. She won't be able to keep him. He'll dump her. And then she'll be throwing herself over the side of the ship again, and it'll ruin the whole trip for all of us."

"I'm not worried," Lila said stubbornly. She crossed her arms. "I think you should thank me and quit criticizing. Jared called Ellen and asked for a date. I didn't notice little Mikey asking her out."

Jessica straightened up and put her hands on her hips. "His name is Sam," she said through gritted teeth. "Sam Sloane. And he will ask her for a date at the disco tonight."

"Hah! I'll bet we never even see that guy again," Lila remarked. "He's the type of guy who's so busy being everybody's friend, he doesn't have time to be anybody's friend. He can't even remember Ellen's name."

"He will," Jessica said grimly. "After I get through coaching her."

Back in the cabin, Ellen set Lila's little purse on the dresser then lifted her arm over her head. Boy! Her shoulder was really sore. Not to mention her jaw. That tic stuff was working muscles she didn't know she had.

But Lila had been right about Jared. He was interested. Really interested. And once Ellen got a good look at him, she realized he was handsome— as in drop-dead handsome. She'd never had a guy that good-looking interested in her before.

She'd never had a guy that rich interested in her before, either. Other than Lila, he was the only middle schooler she had ever seen with a credit card. A gold one no less. He'd treated them to brunch at the most expensive restaurant on the island followed by a horse-and-buggy ride through the old part of town.

Appearing bored had been a big effort. Good thing she'd had Lila along to stomp on her toe every time she started to sound enthused or impressed.

Ellen eased her foot out of her sandal. Ick! Her big toe was black and blue.

There was a knock at the door and Jessica swept

in without even waiting for an answer. She had what looked like some clothes draped over her arm. "Take that off and put this on," she commanded.

"Put what on?"

Jessica held up a short flippy red skirt and a white, V-necked cotton sweater with a red trim around the sleeves. Ellen squinted. "You brought your cheerleading outfit on a cruise?"

"It's not a cheerleading outfit!" Jessica snapped.

"It looks like one."

"It's meant to *suggest* a cheerleading outfit," Jessica explained. "It's retro fifties. A fashion thing. *Fashion*. You've heard of it?"

"You don't have to be sarcastic," Ellen complained.

Jessica laid the outfit out on the bed. "It's a little tight on me, so it ought to fit you perfectly. You don't need any hose or anything. Just some tennis shoes. It'll be perfect."

Ellen wrinkled her brow. "I'm confused. Perfect for what?"

"For the dance," Jessica explained. "Sam is going to be there, and I want you to try to make a good impression on him. He's a fantastic guy and I think he'd really be good for you."

Ellen touched the skirt. It even *felt* like cheerleader skirt material. What did Jessica want her to do? Turn somersaults in front of him? Nope. She'd turned enough somersaults for one day. "Thanks but no thanks, Jessica. I've got a guy. Sort of. Jared." She handed the skirt to Jessica.

Jessica put her hand on Ellen's shoulder and shoved, forcing her to sit. "Jared Matthews is a pompous moneybag of wind. I don't want to sound insulting, but frankly, I don't think he's going to be there for you in the long run."

"I'm not planning to get married before college," Ellen quipped. "So I'm not sure that's a concern." She tried to stand but Jessica pushed her back down.

"I mean I don't think he'll be around for the rest of the cruise," Jessica said. "There are a lot of girls on this boat. Jared's a good-looking rich guy. By tonight, he may be history. Then who are you going to dance with? Who are you going to hold hands in the moonlight with? Who . . . "

"I get the picture," Ellen groaned. "You think Sam has more staying power."

"I think he's a totally upbeat and uncritical guy. And I think he'd be happy with any girl who's willing to give him, and life, a chance."

Ellen stood and pretended to play a little violin.

Jessica pointed an accusatory finger in Ellen's face. "That's exactly the kind of thing that's got to stop. You've got to stop moping and sighing and groaning. We're on a cruise. We're in the Caribbean. We've got ten days with no parents. So would you please smile and be happy?" She threw the flippy skirt at Ellen's head. Ellen pushed the pleats aside and smiled as widely as she could.

"That's it," Jessica said encouragingly. "Happy, happy, happy."

Six

Happy, happy, happy. Ellen grinned until her dimples ached. And she didn't even *have* dimples.

The disco was packed. The music was thumping. The lights were flashing. And Ellen and Sam were dancing—their third dance in a row.

The music stalled, skipped a beat, and segued into a song that had been popular back when Ellen was in the fifth grade.

"Oh *wow!*" Sam cried. "I love this song. Remember?" He began clapping his hands in time to the music.

Ellen clapped her own hands and infused every single ounce of enthusiasm she possessed into her ecstatic "Yes! Yes! I remember! It was my favorite!"

Sam threw back his head and howled. "A fantastic song. A superfantastic girl. I love it!"

Ellen threw her head back too. "Life is just sooooo great," she agreed, feeling sort of like an idiot.

She caught Jessica watching her from the perimeter of the dance floor. Jessica smiled and gave Ellen an encouraging nod. Ellen grinned and winked.

What else could she do? It turned out the outfit that Jessica lent her was brand-new. Jessica hadn't even worn it yet. For Jessica, that was as selfless as giving somebody a kidney. The least Ellen could do in return was look like she was having fun.

The music began to slow and Sam took her hand and drew her nearer to him. The song was a ballad called "Heart of Mine," one of Johnny Buck's biggest hits.

Sam put an arm around her waist and the next thing Ellen knew, they were rocking from side to side in an embrace. Sam's face was centimeters from her ear and she could feel his breath. "Wow!" he whispered. "Great perfume."

"I'm sure Ellen had a good time today," Lila said, taking a cup of pineapple and sparkling water punch from the waiter. "Why wouldn't she? I mean, lunch at the St. Simone Princess Hotel and a horse-and-buggy ride through the old part of town. It was a great day."

Jared lifted his square jaw and frowned. "I hope you're right. You know, it's tough to know how to make an impression on a girl like Ellen. She's done so much and seen so much. How do you make a date or an event seem special or out of the ordinary?"

Lila smiled. "What makes a day special is who you spend it with."

Jared's eyes met Lila's and held her gaze. Lila's heart skipped a beat, and for some odd reason, she began to blush. The last few bars of "Heart of Mine" faded away.

Lila hoped Jared wasn't getting interested in *her*. That wasn't the plan at all. It would be a total disaster. Understandable, sure. What guy wouldn't be more interested in Lila than Ellen?

But her mission was to get Jared and Ellen together. So that meant she'd have to work extrahard to keep Jared's attention focused on Ellen and not on her.

She was pleased to see Jared's eyes light up as he spotted Ellen in the crowd. "Here she comes," he said eagerly.

Lila took a sip of her punch and turned. When she saw Ellen, she choked, spewing pineapple and sparkling water punch all over the three guys standing in front of her.

"Oops. Sorry," Lila muttered to the guys, but she was too shocked by the sight of Ellen to be embarrassed. Ellen looked like an idiot. Like a parody of a popular cheerleader.

Ellen let out a loud, braying laugh. "Lila! What's the matter? Did somebody put strychnine in your punch? Hi, Jared." Ellen gave them both a wide smile. "Isn't this the greatest party?" she gushed enthusiastically. "It's like a real disco. And the DJ is a total pro. What a great mix of songs. Especially 'Heart of Mine.'"

Jared was staring at Ellen as if she had suddenly grown two heads.

Lila glared at Ellen over the rim of her cup. *Chill out,* the look said. *You're blowing the act.*

Ellen looked confused at first. Then Lila's message seemed to sink in. Ellen's eyelids fluttered down until they were half closed and she leaned languidly against the wall. She hummed a few bars of "Heart of Mine"—slightly off-key. "That song brings back so many memories. Paris in the summer. We'd sit in the little cafés and listen to Johnny Buck."

"Johnny Buck is popular in Paris?" Jared asked, handing Ellen a cup of punch.

"Oh, yes," Ellen replied. "Johnny Buck is popular all over Europe. And in parts of the Middle East."

"You've been to the Middle East?" Jared whistled. "Wow! How was it?"

"Very sandy," Ellen drawled.

Lila suppressed a groan.

Ellen seemed to decide it was time for a Royal Riteman Tic Attack, because her mouth opened wide and her elbow shot up, sending what was left of her punch over her shoulder. A few drops rained down on Ellen and Jared, but most of it landed on the same three guys that Lila had spewed.

They turned, muttering angrily.

The music started up again. "Would you like to dance, Ellen?" Jared asked quickly.

Ellen yawned. "Why not? We're here. We're young. There's music. What else is there to do?" She handed her empty cup to Lila and took Jared's arm.

Lila watched Ellen walk slowly out to the dance floor with Jared and felt a slight flicker of irritation. Acting cool was one thing. But Ellen was acting totally snotty. She was taking Jared for granted.

Lila made up her mind to have a talk with Ellen. Jared might be rich and well connected, but that didn't mean he didn't have feelings.

Jessica was near the DJ's booth talking with two girls from San Diego when Sam appeared at her elbow. "Can I talk to you?" he asked, giving the two other girls a smile.

"Sure," she replied, feeling a little bewildered as he took her arm and pulled her a few feet away. "Where's Ellen? I thought you two were dancing."

"We were," Sam said. "But when the DJ took a break, Ellen said she wanted to say hi to somebody so I went over to say hello to a friend from school. The next thing I know, she's dancing with him." Sam nodded toward the dance floor.

Jessica frowned. "That's Jared. He's a friend of Lila's."

"I know. He was at dinner last night. But I guess what I'm asking is, does Ellen like him? I mean, does it mean anything that they're dancing together?" Sam looked slightly worried. "I'd sort of like to cut in, but I don't want to if there's something going on there."

"Oh nooooo," Jessica said immediately. She put her hand on Sam's arm meaning to give it a little push. "I think you should cut in. Definitely. In fact, I think you should cut in as soon as possible."

Jessica pushed him harder than she'd intended. And Sam went careening onto the dance floor.

"Oommmphhh!" Ellen cried when somebody collided with her from behind.

Jared looked irritated, and Ellen turned. Her assailant was Sam. He looked momentarily flustered, then he pushed his bangs back and began to laugh. "Wow! How was that for an entrance?"

Jared looked less than amused. Ellen curbed her impulse to laugh and gave Sam an icy smile.

"May I cut in?" Sam said to Jared.

Ellen's mouth fell open slightly. Sam was cutting in on Jared. There were actually *two* guys who wanted to dance with her. This was a first.

Jared's face darkened slightly. Ellen wondered for a moment if he was going to refuse. But Jared

Matthews was nothing if not a gentleman. What could he do? He smiled at Ellen, reluctantly released her hand, and melted into the crowd.

Sam took her hand. "This is my all-time favorite sixties tune," he said. "I had to dance to it with you."

"Sixties music is cute," Ellen murmured in a wan tone.

Sam's beaming face looked slightly crestfallen. "You don't like sixties music?"

Ellen shrugged. "I suppose I do. I just long for something fresh every once and a while. Fresh places and fresh faces."

"Gee! Well." Sam let go of her hand. "I didn't realize you were getting bored with me. Sorry to butt in." He turned and walked quickly away.

Ellen watched him walk away wishing she could fall through a hole in the floor. She hadn't meant it that way. Actually, she hadn't meant it *any* way. It was just part of her rich girl act. She'd forgotten to turn it off. She hadn't meant to hurt his feelings. "Sam!" she cried.

But the DJ had pumped up the volume and he couldn't hear her.

Jessica stood beside the refreshment table with Mandy and Kimberly. She lifted her soda. "Here's to me. Primo matchmaker. I think Ellen and Sam are a sure thing." She laughed. "Can you believe Lila? Trying to match up Ellen and that Jared guy?"

"I think you're both nuts," Mandy said irritably. "Neither one is Ellen's type."

"Mandy's right." Kimberly nibbled on a cookie. "Who'd want either one of those characters?"

"Sam is not a character," Jessica said angrily. "And . . . "

She broke off. Mandy's and Kimberly's faces had suddenly taken on the look that said whoever was being discussed was within earshot.

A finger tapped her on the shoulder. It was Sam. And his face looked drawn. No trace of a smile anywhere. "Sam. What's wrong?" she cried.

"Can I talk to you for a second?" He took Jessica's hand and led her a few feet away. "Did I really goof by cutting in on Ellen?"

"No! Why?"

"Because she really gave me the cold shoulder."

"Cold shoulder?" Jessica repeated.

"Yeah. She was totally bored and disinterested. It was sooo weird. She changed . . . " He snapped his fingers. "Just like that. Fifteen minutes ago, she was totally enthused and having a fab time. Now she's tired of my face."

Only by exercising superhuman effort was Jessica able to keep from screaming. Lila! She was behind this. And Ellen was stupid enough to listen to her.

Jessica looked around, trying to decide who to yell at—Lila or Ellen.

She spotted Ellen first. Heading into the ladies'
room.

"I'll be back," she said sweetly to Sam. "Wait
here and don't worry about a thing."

"Are you out of your mind?" Jessica hissed, cutting in line so that she could stand behind Ellen.

Ellen screeched and jumped. "Do you have to
sneak up on me?"

Jessica grabbed the back of Ellen's T-shirt and
pulled her back behind the crowd and over by the
sinks. "What are you trying to do? Chase off the
greatest guy that ever happened to you? Sam's feelings are really hurt."

"I got confused," Ellen protested. "One minute I
was dancing with Jared, the next minute I was
dancing with Sam. It's hard going from Ms. Been-
there-done-that to being The-happiest-girl-in-the-
whole-USA.

"Well get a grip," Jessica warned. "Sam is . . .
Hold it! What's that?"

Ellen looked around. "What's what?"

Jessica pointed to a large spot on the front of
Ellen's skirt. "That? What is that spot on my skirt?"

"Punch, I think. Sorry." She grabbed a paper
towel, wet it in the sink, and dabbed at the skirt.

"You're just making it worse," Jessica said nervously. "Look. The dance is almost over. I'll tell
Sam you weren't feeling well. You go back to the

cabin and take it off and hang it up. There's a dry cleaner on Deck 1. I'll take it first thing in the morning. And *smile!*"

"So she's not mad?" Sam ran a nervous hand over his chin.

When Jessica had come out of the ladies' room, she had found Sam hovering nearby, waiting for Jessica to come back with her report.

Jessica took his hands and pulled him away from the crowd, so that his back was to the ladies' room door.

Jessica watched Ellen sneak out of the ladies' room and dart toward the disco exit behind him.

"No, no. She's just not feeling well. You know Ellen. Go, go, go! Never wants to miss a minute of fun. But she doesn't know her own limits and she gets worn out. She went back to her cabin to rest."

"Already?" Sam frowned. "But I never saw her come out of the . . . "

"That's Ellen," Jessica chirped, watching the exit door shut behind her friend. "She moves so fast, if you blink, you miss her."

Sam turned a perplexed face toward the ladies' room again. Then he shook his head. "I guess you're right." He turned his attention back toward Jessica. "But she does want to see me again?"

"Oh, yes," Jessica said, putting a reassuring hand on his arm. "She thinks you're *fantastic!*"

*   *   *

Lila shook her head incredulously when she spotted Mandy dancing with Jack, the guy she'd brought to dinner last night. Jack had on black jeans, a black sweatshirt and a black bandanna on his head. One thing was clear: Mandy's taste in guys was almost as bad as Jessica's. What kind of idiot walked around on a cruise ship in the middle of summer wearing black? Probably a New Yorker or somebody trying to look like one.

"Can I talk to you?" she said to Mandy, not bothering to acknowledge Jack. Who wanted to get into a long conversation with somebody like that?

"I'll see you later," Mandy told Jack.

"Thanks for the dance," Jack replied. "We'll talk more about that little matter later . . . "

Lila led Mandy off the dance floor. "What *little matter* is Zorro talking about?"

"Don't be sarcastic about Jack," Mandy warned. "And if you must know, we were talking about Ellen. He's a great guy for Ellen. He's very sensitive."

Lila blinked her eyes. "Listen, Mandy. I've got the guy thing covered. And if you and Jessica would just butt out . . . "

"Excuuuuuuuseee me." Jessica came up to them, looking peeved. "If anybody's going to butt out, it ought to be you. Would you please call off your overpedigreed hound?"

"Would you please quit encouraging Ellen to act like a game show contestant who just won some tacky set of dining room furniture," Lila retorted. She grinned stupidly and bounced around. "It's all sooooo fantastic! Fab! Wonderful!" she shrieked in a squeaky voice.

Mandy giggled.

"She's acting like an idiot," Lila finished in disgusted voice. "She's acting like . . . "

"Me?" Jessica asked.

"I didn't say that," Lila retorted.

"But that's what you meant, wasn't it?" Jessica pressed.

Lila pursed her lips. Jessica was right. That was what she meant. "Well, maybe it was. But don't blame me for the fact that you have to act so super upbeat about everything."

Jessica narrowed her eyes. "Well, if you think Ellen looks stupid acting like me, how do you think she looks when she's acting like you?" she countered.

"Cut it out," Mandy ordered. "People are starting to stare. If we get into a big fight, we're going to look stupid. Let's keep our eye on the goal. Find Ellen a guy so *we* can feel OK about spending the cruise with guys. Right?"

"Right," Lila admitted.

"OK then," Mandy said. "Let Ellen make up her own mind about who's right for her, and then let's get on with the party."

Lila looked around. Only a few people were left in the big disco. The refreshment table had been completely ravaged, and stewards were beginning to clear away the large trays.

"I think the party's over," Mandy said. "Let's find Kimberly and head back to the cabin."

Ellen zipped up her jeans and reached for her Sweet Valley Middle School T-shirt, pulling it over her head. She was totally pooped. And totally confused. In fact, she felt a little like she was developing multiple personality disorder.

But she had two really great guys interested in her. So it was worth it—wasn't it?

Ellen clipped Jessica's skirt to the hanger and hung it in the bathroom so the wrinkles could fall out. She paused in front of the mirror. Her makeup looked clownish and unreal in the harsh light. Especially with her jeans and T-shirt. She turned on the tap and began washing her face.

The little doorbell to the cabin buzzed. Ellen figured it was Lila. Her disco bag was so small, she probably didn't have room in it for her key.

Ellen went to the door. "Dahhhhhhling," she joked. But when she pulled the door open, it wasn't Lila.

It was Curtis.

"*Rabies!*" he screamed, pointing at her face.

"What?" Ellen touched her cheek in alarm. It

was still covered with lather. "It's OK," she hastened to explain. "I was just washing—"

Curtis removed some lather from her chin and held his hand in front of her. "Pretty cool soap bubble. Do you want to pop it or should I?"

Ellen looked up at him. He had the funniest twinkle in his eye. "Let's both pop it," she suggested.

He held up his hand and she slapped him a high five.

"Awesome job!" Curtis exclaimed.

Ellen giggled and motioned him to come in.

He collapsed into the chair beside the dresser while Ellen went into the bathroom and rinsed off her face. She patted it dry with a towel and went back out.

Curtis let out a hiccup, and then pointed to the bag on his lap. "Real food," he explained. He reached in and pulled out a bag of Cheesy Thingdos, a bag of Chocolate Cream Dream Cookies, and a variety of candy bars. "Man! Did you see that stuff on the buffet? I'm not sure I can survive ten days at sea on that stuff. Bleehhh."

Ellen sat down on the floor and Curtis slid down next to her. "So how was the dance?"

Exhausting. Humiliating. Crazifying, Ellen thought. "OK," she answered, opening the bag of cookies and feeling thankful she didn't have to smile like a hyena or drawl like a debutante. "I didn't see you there."

"I peeked in a couple of times. But you were always dancing with somebody so I went to a movie. Wow! It was awesome. Some dude with a camera followed this other dude while he went snorkeling. Awesome fish."

"Sounds great," Ellen said. "I'm sorry I missed it." She really was. Sitting in a nice dark movie theater looking at fish with Curtis Bowman sounded very relaxing. Sitting anywhere with Curtis was relaxing. He was a relaxing guy. Maybe because *he* was so relaxed. Ellen suddenly realized her shoulders were no longer up around her ears.

"No problem. They show it every night. I could dig seeing it again. Maybe we could catch it tomorrow or . . . "

The door flew open.

"Well!" breathed a disapproving voice at the door.

Ellen and Curtis both jumped guiltily.

Lila, Jessica, Mandy, and Kimberly crowded in the doorway. They looked shocked. And disappointed. Like parents who'd just caught their kids sneaking in after curfew.

"Hey, man," Curtis said. "We're just havin' a snack. Want some?"

"I'd appreciate it if you'd *snack* someplace else," Lila said to Curtis. "I really don't want junk food crumbs scattered all over my cabin, thank you."

"Lila's right," Jessica said. "It's common

knowledge that ships have *rats.*" When she said the word *rats* she gave Curtis a pointed look.

Ellen felt her face burn. Lila was rude to everybody, so her behavior wasn't that big a deal. But Jessica was really going out of her way to be insulting. And Mandy was just standing by and letting her do it. So was Kimberly. Why were they being so awful?

"What is your problem?" she demanded. "You guys sound like prison guards or something."

Curtis stood and bobbed his head. He picked up the sack and smiled. "Good thing it's a movable feast. Want to go sit in the video arcade?" he asked Ellen.

"She can't," Kimberly said flatly. "We've got some stuff we have to do."

"What?" Ellen demanded.

"We need to have a meeting," Mandy answered. She turned to Curtis. "We're a club. The Unicorn Club. We can't have a meeting without our president. And Ellen is our president."

"Our meetings are private," Lila said nastily. "So you don't mind leaving, do you? Now?"

Curtis nodded. "That's cool! I understand. Sure. So . . . I'll see you around. Have a good meeting." He gave Ellen a wave as he sidled past her four, very hostile friends.

Ellen was so stunned, she could barely find her voice. "Thanks for coming by," she managed to choke.

As soon as Curtis was out the door, Jessica kicked it closed with the back of her foot. "We've got to talk."

Ellen was so angry and upset, her hands shook. A lump rose in her throat and she swallowed hard, fighting tears. "We sure do. Curtis will probably never speak to me again and I wouldn't blame him. How dare you? How *dare* you be so mean and rude to him? What kind of friends are you?"

"We did that *because* we're your friends," Lila said. "Can't you see that?"

Jessica disappeared into the bathroom. Ellen saw her inspect her skirt. "We care about you. We want you to be happy." Jessica took it off the bathroom rack and emerged with it over her shoulder. "That guy is bad news. A total phony. You shouldn't be encouraging guys like that to hang around you."

"They'll make you look bad," Kimberly agreed.

Mandy took Ellen's hand and sat down on the end of the bed. "We really do care about you, Ellen. We know it's been a bad time with your parents' divorce and all. And we know you're vulnerable. So we're looking out for you. That's what friends are for. Right?"

Jessica leaned back into the bathroom, pulled a tissue from the dispenser, and handed it to Ellen.

Ellen wiped away the tears that trickled down her cheek. Two seconds ago she'd been furious, and now she felt guilty for being angry. After all, the Unicorns *were* going to a lot of trouble on her behalf. Instead of being resentful, she ought to be grateful. "Thanks," Ellen said quietly. "It's nice to know you care."

"We do care," Mandy said.

"I'll get up early and meet Jared for breakfast," Lila said briskly. "I'll tell him you didn't feel well and left early but you'd love to get together with him again."

Jessica rustled her skirt on the hanger to shake out the creases. "And I'll find Sam and tell him you're really excited about getting together with him too."

"Then you can make up your own mind about who's right for you," Mandy said.

Seven

Ellen snuggled down deeper under the covers. She'd slept heavily. And she'd dreamed all night. She'd dreamed about Jared. And Sam. And Curtis.

But in her dreams, they kept getting mixed up. She was never sure who was who.

Ellen kept getting herself mixed up in the dream too. Sometimes she was Ellen. But sometimes she was Jessica. And sometimes she was Lila.

It was all very confusing.

She opened her eyes. What time was it?

The sun was streaming in the porthole and Lila's bed was empty. Her nightgown and robe (purchased from Maria's Secret Love) lay on the floor like a puddle of green silk. The closet door was open and so was the top bureau drawer.

Ellen frowned. Lila had gotten dressed and gone to breakfast without her. How come?

Then she remembered.

Lila was schmoozing Jared over breakfast. And Jessica was schmoozing Sam.

Ellen's stomach rumbled. She pictured the mouthwatering selection of muffins, pastries, and fruit that was served at breakfast. Poppy seed muffins. Cranberry muffins. Cheese Danish.

There was a muffled knock. Ellen sprang up. Maybe Lila or Jessica had brought her back something from the dining room. She threw open the door. But it wasn't Lila or Jessica providing room service. It was Mandy.

Mandy came in quickly and furtively, as though she was worried somebody was spying on her. She closed the door quietly behind her.

Ellen noticed she had something bundled up in her arms. But it didn't look like muffins. "I told Jack we'd meet him for breakfast in half an hour," Mandy said.

"Jack?"

"He's wonderful," Mandy continued. "An artist. A painter and a jewelry maker. And so sensitive. He actually writes poetry. He understands what people are feeling and he cares. I think he'd be a great guy for you."

Ellen shook her head. Maybe this was some kind of weird seasickness that produced delusions or hallucinations or something. Was that really Mandy standing in Ellen's cabin waving a tie-dyed dress like a matador's cape and giving some guy a rave review? Couldn't be.

Ellen rubbed her eyes and looked again.

Yep. It was Mandy. "Correct me if I'm wrong," Ellen said, "but weren't you the one who said I should make up my own mind about who's right for me?"

"Sure," Mandy said. "But how can you decide before you've seen all the choices." She unrolled the bundle in her arms, unfurling a tie-dyed dress as if it were a flag. "I thought this looked like a good breakfast-at-sea dress."

Ellen eyed it. "Didn't you make that especially for this trip?"

"Yes," Mandy said. "But I don't see any reason to mention that to Jack. In fact, I sort of told him that *you* made a lot of my clothes and yours."

Ellen groaned and flopped backward on the bed. "Anything else I should know about me?"

Mandy began to empty her pockets, producing jewelry, hairpins, and various makeup items. "Yes. You make stained glass. And your hobbies are modern dance and writing poetry. What do you think about this lipstick color?" She pulled the top off of a silver cylinder.

Ellen stared at the lipstick for a moment, struggling for words. She wasn't suffering from some weird seasickness. But apparently Mandy was. "It's *black*," Ellen pointed out gently.

Mandy grinned. "I know. Isn't that cool?"

Ellen twirled along the outer deck, letting Mandy's full gauzy skirt sway around her ankles. Mandy had pinned her hair up in a loose twirl and lent her some dangling sea-glass earrings she had made.

"Roses are red, violets are blue," Ellen breathed in what she hoped was an arty voice. "June, spoon, moon, goon, loon, tune, croon, noon, soon . . ."

"Cut it out," Mandy snapped.

Ellen couldn't help snorting a laugh. "*You* cut it out. You're interfering with my creative process. I'm trying to compose a poem." Ellen couldn't believe Mandy was actually serious about this charade. Couldn't she see how totally ridiculous it was?

Ellen gazed out to sea, crossed her eyes, and folded her hands over her breast. "Sea, me, tea, bee . . ."

Mandy turned and gazed at Ellen with a wounded expression. "This is really important to me, Ellen. Jack is a very sensitive and serious guy. If you act like you're making fun of poetry and art, you'll hurt his feelings."

"Sorry," Ellen said immediately. She felt a little guilty again. Mandy was a truly nice person. Ellen would never do anything to hurt her if she could help it. If it was important to Mandy that Ellen act artistic, then by golly, she'd act artistic. "I'll be good," Ellen promised. "But he's not going to expect me to talk in rhymes or anything, is he?"

Mandy's tense face relaxed. "Just be yourself. And everything will be fine." She squeezed Ellen's hand. "Here's Jack now."

Jack came hurrying down the stairwell to meet them. He had on faded black cutoffs, a faded black T-shirt, and slip-on black Keds with no socks. His hair was pulled back and caught in a ponytail. An earring similar to the ones Ellen wore hung from his ear.

"Did you *see* that sunrise this morning?" he asked them.

"No," Mandy said. "But Ellen did. In fact, she was just describing it to me."

Jack gave Ellen a brilliant smile. "Really? I'd love to hear your description. Mandy says you're a poet. I scribble a little myself." He brushed a loose lock of dark hair back from his large, liquid brown eyes. "Come on, let's get our breakfast and bring it back outside." He turned and started into the dining room.

Sun, bun, done, fun, gun, none . . . , Ellen thought wildly as the dining room door opened and the crosswind caused her gauzy skirt to billow gracefully.

* * *

"I'll get some more jelly," Sam said. "Anybody else want anything?"

"Some marmalade would be great," Jessica answered. Sam got up and moved through the crowded dining room toward the buffet.

Jessica had met Sam in the dining room early. She had had just enough time to reassure him about Ellen when Lila and Jared had come walking in.

When they sat down with Jessica and Sam, Lila had thrown Jessica a smug smile. Jessica figured the smile meant Lila had already given Jared the big Ellen pitch and he was still interested.

Jessica wasn't worried, though. She'd convinced Sam to hang in there.

The dining room was already packed with people. A line had formed at both ends of the buffet table.

"I want another muffin," Jared said. "Lila, can I get you anything?"

"Nothing, thank you," Lila said with a gentle smile.

Jared stood and headed toward the buffet table.

Lila kept smiling until Jared moved out of sight. Then she fixed Jessica with a steely look. "I can't believe you think Sam is right for Ellen," she hissed.

"And I can't believe you think Jared is right," Jessica shot back. "Uggghhh!" Jessica found Jared so incredibly irritating, she didn't know how she'd manage to sit at the table with him. He was a hundred times worse than Lila. Brag, brag, brag, brag. In the course of one muffin and one glass of juice, he'd managed to mention that his family owned houses in Palm Springs, Vail, and Los Angeles. That his father played polo. That his mother had been to tea with a real countess, and that his grandfather had promised him the car of his choice as soon as he was old enough to get a license.

He was as full of himself as Lila. No wonder she thought he was so great.

Kimberly slid into the seat next to Lila, her plate loaded with fruit, cereal, and a glass of juice. "*What is Ellen doing in that ridiculous getup?*" she demanded angrily.

"Ellen?" Jessica repeated blankly. "What are you talking about?"

"Ellen's in the cabin. Asleep," Lila said.

"No she's not." Kimberly pointed toward the buffet table on the right. "She's over there. In line with Mandy."

Jessica and Lila both turned to look.

It was all Jessica could do not to scream. On a one to ten irritation meter, she was registering somewhere around sixteen. What was Ellen thinking? What was Mandy trying to do? Didn't Jessica have enough problems getting Sam and Ellen together without *this?*

"She looks like she's wearing a Halloween

costume," Lila wailed. "All she needs is a trick-or-treat bag."

"I can't believe this," Kimberly said. "I got up really early to play handball with Peter, who, by the way, is the greatest guy in the world. Totally centered. Totally focused. Really into healthy mind, healthy body stuff. I spent forty minutes telling him what a down-to-earth and health-oriented girl Ellen is—and now look at her! I can't let him see her looking like that. She looks like a vampire."

"We can't let *anybody* see her looking like that," Lila squeaked.

Jessica watched, horrified, as Sam moved toward Ellen, Mandy, and Jack from the left, and Jared moved toward Ellen, Mandy, and Jack from the right. They were on a collision course.

"Oh, no," Lila croaked. "It's all over." She lifted her napkin and covered her eyes. "I can't watch."

But Jessica couldn't take her eyes off the scene. It was like watching a wreck. She wanted to close her eyes, but the morbid fascination was just too strong to resist.

Ellen, Mandy, and Jack paused in front of the juice glasses, lingering over their selection.

Jessica's heartbeat slowed to a sickening thud and then stopped when she realized that Sam had gotten his jelly and left the line on the left *just as* Jared got his muffin and left the line on the right.

Jessica's heart went back to work, pounding

away as both boys missed the spectacle of Ellen and Company leaving the dining room looking like creatures of the night about to venture into the day.

"It's OK," Jessica breathed. She felt giddy with relief. "They missed each other."

"Are they coming to sit over here?" Lila asked.

"No . . . no . . . it looks like they're going out to sit on the deck."

Lila lowered her napkin and let out a sigh of relief. "We're saved."

"What am I supposed to tell Peter?" Kimberly demanded.

Jessica picked up a piece of Danish and nibbled the edge. "Tell him she got sick."

"After I spent all that time telling him how healthy she is? No way." Kimberly stood up, dropping her napkin. "You two are no help. I'll have to think of something myself and head him off at the pass. But I am definitely going to set up a tennis date for him and Ellen and don't try to stop me. You know, I never realized until this trip that you guys and Mandy have the absolute *worst* taste in guys."

Kimberly stomped off.

"Well!" Jessica said. "Of all the nerve. *You* may have bad taste in guys. And Mandy might have bad taste in guys. But *my* taste is impeccable. Sam Sloane is a catch."

"Jared Matthews is a prince," Lila retorted.

Jessica caught a glimpse of white blond hair hanging down the back of a bilious green and purple Hawaiian shirt. She shuddered. "And Curtis Bowman is a frog."

"Well, at least we all agree on something," Lila said, reaching for her juice.

Eight

Later that morning, Ellen squinted in the sunlight as the tennis ball came hurtling toward her. She drew back her racket and leaned into the swing. The ball connected with her racket, dead center. She placed it with her follow-through.

The ball whizzed over the net, clearing it by less than two inches.

"Good shot!" Peter shouted as he ran backward to return it. He swung his racket and lobbed it back toward Ellen.

Ellen looked up, watching the arching ball as she ran. It had begun its downward descent.

She ran beyond the white line and positioned herself, waiting for the ball to land. She drew back her racket and watched the ball bounce—a good four inches *outside* the white line.

Very quickly, she reviewed her options. She could yell *"out,"* take the point, and win the game—which would put them five all for the set. But then they'd have to play again to break the tie.

On the other hand, she could try to return the shot, hit it into the net, and let him win the game.

Kimberly had lent her tennis shoes, a tennis dress, and her tennis racket. All of it was top of the line equipment. Ellen wasn't a bad player, but she really didn't enjoy the game. Running. Sweating. Chasing a ball around. And for what?

Ellen deliberately angled her racket in order to hit the ball with the edge.

Thwack!

The ball shot sideways at an odd angle and bounced against the chain-link fence that surrounded the court. Ellen threw up her arm and racket in a gesture of defeat, then bowed.

Peter laughed, ran up to the net, and jumped over it. "Well played," he said in a pleased voice. "Kimberly was right—you *are* a good player."

"Well . . ." Ellen smiled modestly. "I try."

"Let's get something to drink," Peter suggested, gesturing toward the benches alongside the court, where jugs of lemonade and thirst quencher were set out for the players.

Peter took two plastic cups from the dispenser. "You like thirst quencher, right? Lemonade's full of refined sugar, and Kimberly says you're very health-conscious." He filled two cups and handed one to Ellen. "Time to replenish the old electrolytes." He tapped his cup against Ellen's before gulping his drink down. Then squashed his cup and dropped it into a wastebasket. "Come on. Let's have lunch."

What are electrolytes? Ellen followed Peter to a table at the Spa Café, a little outdoor luncheon area set up a few yards from the tennis court. They sat down and a waiter came over. "The spa plate?" Peter asked her.

"Um . . . sure," Ellen replied. Whatever. She took a sip of her thirst quencher.

The waiter nodded and disappeared.

Peter leaned forward. "So how long have you been playing?"

"I can't really remember," she muttered. "A long time, I guess." Ellen tried not to seem bored. Playing tennis was OK, but it wasn't the most interesting thing to talk about.

"Me too. I've been into athletics ever since I was a kid," Peter said. "My dad was actually an Olympic runner one year. Won a silver medal. Then he finished college and got his Ph.D. in history. He teaches at UCLA. I like history, but I like math and science too. What about you? What's your favorite subject?"

Ellen took a sip of her thirst quencher—though

why she forced herself to drink it she didn't know. What was in this stuff? It tasted like flat soda and it had the consistency of liquid soap.

"Hard to pick *one?*" Peter laughed. "I guess you really *are* a studious person. You like every subject. That's great. Really, really great. It's important to be well-rounded. So many kids are into sports and nothing else. Or they're into school and nothing else. Or into one subject—and that's it."

Ellen didn't really have anything to say about that. She wasn't overly interested in any *one* thing. She wasn't really very interested in *anything.*

"I'm into balance," Peter continued. "That's my thing. Intellectual and physical balance. Would you consider yourself balanced?"

"Oh yeah," Ellen said. "Definitely." She was balanced, all right. She was equally disinterested in everything.

"You're just going to confuse her," Lila said angrily to Kimberly.

Lila, Mandy, Jessica, and Kimberly were all having lunch in the main dining room. The windows were open on both sides and low-hanging ceiling fans circulated the fresh sea air. The buffet of fresh fruit, sandwiches, and chopped vegetables was as elegant as any buffet Lila had ever seen.

If Lila hadn't been so totally annoyed at everybody, she would have been thoroughly content.

"*I'm* going to confuse her," Kimberly sputtered. "How do you figure that?"

"Jared and Sam are already interested in her," Lila pointed out. "I think that's enough guys for Ellen to cope with."

"What about Jack?" Mandy demanded.

"Oh *pulllease!*" Lila rolled her eyes. "Mandy, *you* might be able to carry off black lipstick, but Ellen? And what kind of guy likes black lipstick anyway?"

Mandy buttered her roll with small, quick, angry movements. "Jack is an extremely talented and sensitive guy, and he happens to be interested in Ellen. He told me so after breakfast."

"Ellen doesn't want some guy like that," Kimberly said, grimacing. She scraped the mayo off her sandwich. "Would somebody please tell me where it's written that sandwiches *have* to have mayo on them?" she muttered irritably. "Don't they know this stuff is poison?"

"Why *wouldn't* Ellen want a guy like Jack?" Mandy said, her chin quivering.

"That first night at dinner?" Kimberly said, raising her eyebrow like she just couldn't believe what she was about to say. "You know what he talked about for like, ten minutes? Scenery." She rolled her eyes upward and began to speak in a breathy, theatrical voice. "The grass where he lives isn't quite hunter green, but almost. Except at dusk, when the shadows make the colors deeper. Then it's more of a sage green. Can you believe that? I mean, get real. How much of that could you listen to? Sage. Hunter. Who cares?"

Mandy put her butter knife down with a loud clatter. "You think *Peter* is a brilliant conversationalist." Mandy lowered her jaw and squared her shoulders, trying to look like a guy. "Very few people realize just how important a balanced diet is. It's amazing how many people will eat a baked potato for dinner and think they've had a very healthy meal. But if they tried to study for very long after that, they would fall asleep. Why? Because they haven't fueled their body. And you cannot have a healthy mind without a healthy body."

Lila burst out laughing. "He *said* that?"

"He said that," Mandy confirmed.

"So what?" Kimberly said. "It's true. I mean, we learned that in Life Sciences."

"Who wants to date a Life Sciences teacher?" Mandy demanded.

"Not me," Jessica said. "But I wouldn't want to date Jack, Jared, *or* Peter. I'm telling you, Sam is the only decent pick."

Lila groaned. "Jared Matthews is a once in a lifetime opportunity. If Ellen doesn't see that, she doesn't deserve him."

"Peter makes them all look like lightweights," Kimberly insisted, removing the cheese from her sandwich and replacing it with carrot slices.

"It's Ellen's choice," Mandy reminded them.

"Let's hope she makes it soon," Lila said grumpily. "Because the sooner we get Ellen fixed up, the sooner we can concentrate on finding guys for ourselves."

"Take the ancient Greeks. They really understood the value of combining physical exercise and intellectual stimulation. They had a fascinating civilization . . ."

Ellen leaned against the rail, looking out over the ocean. Gentle waves made white ripples on the surface and every once in a while, something silvery leaped into the air and then disappeared back into the water.

Peter's voice droned on, blending in with the low hum of the engine and the rhythmic lapping of the water against the side of the ship. On various decks, guys and girls played volleyball, swam, sunned themselves, and chatted. Snatches of conversations and laughter floated toward her on the wind, mingling with caws of the gulls that wheeled overhead.

Suddenly, she had the feeling she was being watched. She turned, put her hand over her eyes to block the sun, and looked upward to see if she was nuts.

No. She wasn't. On the topmost deck, leaning over, she saw Curtis. He was shirtless. Even from three decks down, she could see that he was a lot more muscular than he appeared to be in his big floppy shirts.

She started to lift her hand and wave, but stopped when she realized that Peter had asked her a question and was waiting for a response. "Ellen?" he prompted.

"I-I'm sorry," she stuttered. "I was looking at the gulls and got distracted. What did you say?"

"I was asking you if you'd like to go jogging tomorrow afternoon and then go to a lecture. Captain Jackson is giving a talk on the history of shipbuilding and showing some slides from his military career."

Ellen thought about it.

Jogging?

Yuck.

A lecture on the history of shipbuilding?

Double yuck.

Voluntarily spending time with Captain Jackson?

Triple yuck.

Not exactly her first entertainment choice.

Three girls came strolling in their direction. Actually, it was the third time they'd strolled past. They were obviously taking a walk around the deck. Ellen wondered why they kept walking around and around the same deck. It seemed like it would get boring.

As the girls walked by, Ellen realized *why* they kept walking around and around the same deck. They liked the scenery.

Peter was tall, tan, and well muscled. His thick, curly, honey blond hair grew in a V down the back of his neck and dark lashes fringed his large blue eyes.

Peter was boring. But he was a hunk who could pass for a Greek god himself.

The girls slowed slightly as they passed Ellen and Peter. Ellen noticed the sidelong glances at Peter, followed by the appraising stare at Ellen.

Yeah. That's right. He's with me. Believe it and die.

It was a novel experience being the object of envy. Exhilarating even. Ellen searched her memory. Had anything like this ever happened to her before?"

Nope.

But she had to admit, it was a thrill having people be jealous of her. It probably didn't say much for her character. But she'd never claimed to have any character.

Turning down an invitation from a guy who looked like Peter would be an insane thing to do—even if it was an invitation to go jogging and then look at slides from the Battle of the Bulge or something.

Besides, if she said no, Kimberly would kill her.

"If she says no, I'll kill her," Lila hissed.

"You shouldn't be opening Ellen's mail," Mandy protested.

The girls had just come back to Lila's cabin to wait for Ellen. When Lila had opened the door, she had found a note on the floor. A sealed note. Apparently, someone had slid it under the door.

"I have a right to open mail addressed to Ellen if it's from Jared," Lila argued.

Mandy let out an outraged shriek. "No way."

"Way," Lila argued. "I got them together. The relationship is my responsibility. I have a right to know what's going on."

"So what is going on?" Jessica demanded.

"He's inviting Ellen to dinner and dancing tomorrow night—in the VIP club." Lila smirked. She ran over to the closet and began rummaging through her clothes.

You'd think she *was going,* Jessica thought, watching Lila flip through the row of dresses.

The VIP club was a very expensive extra. None of the girls, including Lila, had paid the extra fee to belong. Membership allowed patrons to dine in the captain's private dining room. According to the brochure, the VIP club was usually attended only by the children of U.S. presidents, foreign dignitaries, movie stars, and millionaires.

Kimberly sat down on the bed. "Well, I think Peter, Jack, and Sam are out of the running."

"They've definitely been outclassed," Mandy agreed. "I hope Jack isn't too disappointed. Something like this could really affect his art. He could get blocked and not be able to create anything."

Jessica sat on the end of the bed. "Poor Sam."

Lila pulled her red satin slip dress out of the closet. "This!" she said.

Jessica moaned. The very dress she'd had her eye on. "Poor me," she amended.

"What's going on in here?" Ellen appeared in the doorway swinging her tennis racket.

"You're going to dinner tomorrow night at the VIP club," Lila told her. She held the dress up against Ellen. "What do you think?" she said to Jessica. "Is the length right?"

A white-gloved ship's steward appeared in the doorway and knocked at the frame. He pushed a little cart with four flower arrangements. "Excuse me. I'm looking for Ms. Riteman."

Ellen turned. "I'm Ellen Riteman."

The steward smiled, removed an arrangement of pink tulips and white baby's breath from his rolling cart, and presented it to her with a flourish. "These are for you."

Ellen backed away slightly. Like Snow White from the apple. "I think there's probably some mistake," she muttered in a nervous voice.

Jessica took the flowers from the steward and shoved them into Ellen's arms, forcing her to drop her racket.

Ellen clutched the vase briefly to her chest, and then placed it on the dresser.

"Open the card," Jessica urged. She plucked the little envelope from the ribbon and handed it to Ellen.

Ellen stared at it in openmouthed wonder. Slowly, she peeled the tiny white envelope open and removed the card. "Jared," she gasped.

Jessica, Kimberly, and Mandy all groaned.

Lila pumped her fist victoriously. "Do I know guys or do I know guys?"

"And where would you like these, Ms. Riteman?" the steward asked.

Jessica's eyes widened. The steward was bringing in a second arrangement. Orchids, floating in a cut-glass bowl.

"Those are for me too?" Ellen gasped.

The steward nodded.

"On the dresser, I guess." Ellen moved Jared's arrangement over a bit.

Jessica plucked the card from the bowl and opened it before Ellen could make a move.

"How about gallery hopping on Claire Isle. Tomorrow morning. Jack," Jessica read out loud.

Mandy smiled triumphantly at Lila. "Jack! I should have known. Who else would send something that artistic? So much nicer than a bunch of stems jammed down into that tacky green stuff at the bottom of a vase."

"Are you calling Jared's arrangement tacky?" Lila demanded.

"And these?" the steward interrupted, holding out a potted African violet in one hand and a tall vase with long yellow sunflowers in the other hand.

"Those are for Ellen too?" Jessica croaked.

Ellen sat down at the foot of the bed and shook her head, as if she were having a dizzy spell.

Lila plopped down next to her, looking even more blown away than Ellen.

Kimberly pulled the notes from each arrangement and opened them. "The African violet is from Peter. 'You're everything Kimberly said you were, and more. Looking forward to tomorrow. Peter.' And the sunflowers are from Sam. 'You're the sunniest girl on the ship. How about going dolphin spotting? We'll have lunch in the launch.'"

Jessica watched Ellen touch each arrangement, trailing her fingers along soft petals and lacy leaves. Jared's tulips. Sam's sunflowers. Peter's violet. And Jack's orchids.

Ellen's face was soft. Her eyes were dreamy and unfocused. She was actually humming slightly, with a secretive smile playing at the edges of her mouth.

Somebody had made Ellen very happy.

The question was: Who?

Kimberly looked at Mandy.

Mandy looked at Lila.

Lila looked at Jessica.

And Jessica looked at Ellen.

"Well?" Jessica asked after a long pause. "Who's it going to be?"

Ellen blinked. "Hmmmm?"

"Who's the lucky guy?" Jessica said. "Which invitation are you going to accept?"

"All of them," Ellen answered with a smile.

Then, humming, she disappeared into the bathroom and closed the door.

Nine

Lila opened the guidebook. "Where do we want to start?" she asked. Lila, Mandy, Jessica, and Kimberly were finishing their breakfast in the main dining room and preparing to take the tender to Claire Isle. The tender was what they called the little boat that ferried passengers back and forth from the ship to the island.

The *Caribbean Queen* had docked at Claire Isle this morning before dawn, and the tender left every fifteen minutes.

"What's there to do on Claire Isle?" Jessica asked.

"Lots," Lila answered. "They have shops full of duty-free crystal and china and stuff like that."

"I don't really need any crystal," Kimberly said with a laugh.

"What about a soup tureen?" Mandy joked. "Can't have too many soup tureens."

"OK, OK," Lila said. "So shopping's not where it's at for us. They have lots of art galleries."

"Sounds good to me," Mandy said.

Kimberly and Jessica both made faces and loud noises meant to be snores.

"Then *you* guys pick something to do," Mandy said irritably.

"Let's just go to the island," Lila said. "I'm sure we'll find something we want to do when we get there. It'll be fun just getting off this boat for a while."

Lila closed the guidebook and gathered her things. Her Italian tote bag, her French sunglasses, her German camera, and her Panama hat—bought by her dad *in* Panama. Normally, surrounding herself with expensive things made her feel calm, relaxed, and at peace.

But it wasn't working for her today. She felt closed in. Claustrophobic. And frankly, she was tired of hanging out with Jessica, Mandy, and Kimberly.

She wasn't sick of Ellen—but only because Ellen wasn't ever around. Ellen was always out doing something. Doing something with a guy. While *they* were hanging out in a girl pack.

What's wrong with this picture? Lila thought.

"Wow! Look at this." Jack pulled Ellen's hand and they came to a stop in front of a gallery. The window featured a seven-foot-tall wood carving of a man and a woman standing with their arms draped across each other's shoulders.

"Look at the lines!" Jack exclaimed. "Look at how one line leads logically to the next. How the finish enhances the color of the wood and doesn't cover it."

Ellen stared, trying hard to think of something artistic to say. "It's . . . it's . . . "

"I know exactly what you're trying to say. But it's almost impossible to articulate, isn't it?" Jack finished for her.

Ellen smiled and nodded. One thing she had learned from her lunch with Peter: The less you said, the smarter you seemed. Or if not smarter, then more artistic. Or more aristocratic.

Not that you didn't have to make *some* effort. But she was catching on. Hooking guys was like playing Simon Says.

Only she was playing Jack Says.

If Jack said, "Great use of color," Ellen nodded and said, "Nice tones. Very nice tones."

If Jack stared at a painting and shook his head. Ellen stared at the painting and shook her head too.

All she did was parrot what he said or did, but using slightly different words or gestures.

Jack took her hand and they strolled down the old cobblestone streets. Claire Isle had been colonized by the French, and the narrow streets reminded Ellen a little of the French Quarter in New Orleans: charming pink, yellow, and blue buildings with shuttered windows and wrought iron balconies.

Tropical plants bloomed in pots arranged in doorways and on terraces, and vines clung to and softened the cracked stucco of the old buildings.

At the end of the narrow street, she could see the ocean in the distance. White capped waves curled high and broke as they neared the shore.

Jack twined his fingers through hers as they rounded a corner. Ellen had to admit that the whole experience was pretty romantic.

"Look!" Jack pointed. Ellen turned her head just in time to see a street vendor feed a cracker to the parrot on his shoulder.

Then suddenly, something knocked her off her feet and she fell. A split second later, Jack fell on top of her. Funny. He didn't look like a heavy guy. But he sure felt like a heavy guy.

She heard a series of guttural male "oomphs" and then a familiar voice. "Sorry, dude."

"Curtis?" she managed to wheeze from underneath the pile of bodies.

"Ellen?" Curtis answered from the top.

"Do you two know each other?" Jack asked from the middle.

Somehow, they managed to untangle themselves, and both Jack and Curtis pulled Ellen to her feet.

Curtis bobbed and swayed. "Man! I am soooo sorry. Are you guys OK? I was lookin' at the parrot, you know, and I didn't see you."

"We were looking at the parrot too," Ellen said, dusting herself off. "Jack, this is Curtis."

Curtis smiled and nodded. Jack gave him a thin smile and dusted off his sleeve.

"So are you guys like, sightseeing?" Curtis asked.

Jack rolled his eyes. "What *else* what would be doing?" he asked sarcastically.

Ellen felt a flicker of irritation. After all, Curtis was just trying to make conversation.

Ellen felt sorry for him. She'd said a million dumb things in her life while trying to make conversation.

Curtis swayed. "Well, you could be surfing," he answered as though to say, *what else would you want to do?*

"Are you going surfing?" Jack asked politely.

Curtis shuffled his feet and stuffed his hands down into his pockets. "Nah. The waves are no good. Too tame. So like, what sights have you seen?"

"We've been looking in art galleries," Ellen answered.

"You like art, huh? Cool! What kind?"

Ellen licked her lips nervously. Yikes. A direct question. She didn't really have an answer. She knew there were a lot of different kinds of art. But it all looked pretty much the same to her. Art was . . . well . . . just art. "The kind of art they have here," she said desperately. "Come on, Jack. We'd better hurry. There's a lot more to see before we go back to the ship." She smiled at Curtis. "See you around."

He nodded, bobbed and swayed, giving her the thumbs-up sign.

Ellen practically dragged Jack around the corner. She didn't want Curtis asking her any more questions about her taste in art. It might make it obvious to Jack that she didn't know magenta from Magic Marker.

"Who is that idiot?" Jack asked as they walked past a fountain on their way to another gallery.

Ellen felt an odd pang in her stomach, but she decided to ignore it. "Oh, just somebody I met on the ship," she answered. "Nobody important."

"Talk about a phony." Jack pointed toward the ocean. "Those waves are too tame? Give me a break. Why do guys have to act so macho? It makes us all look bad. People should just be themselves, don't you think?"

"Oh definitely," Ellen answered. *Unless they happen to be Ellen Riteman.*

"There they go again," Lila said, trailing her fingertips in the water of the fountain. The girls sat on the ornate stone of the fountain's edge, sipping fruit drinks served in a coconut shell.

Claire Isle wasn't that large, and it seemed like everywhere the girls went they saw Jack and Ellen going into a gallery or shop or coming out of one.

They had agreed to try to stay out of the way and out of sight to give Ellen and Jack a chance. But it was turning out to be harder than they had anticipated.

Lila watched Ellen and Jack go into one of the native craft shops. "Funny," she said to Mandy. "It's sort of like seeing *you* all over the place."

"Well, sure," Kimberly said, taking a sip of her drink. "She's wearing Mandy's clothes."

Ellen had left the ship this morning wearing one of Mandy's hand-painted baseball hats, three tank tops in red, green, and purple, and a pair of Mandy's baggiest jeans.

Jack had worn his basic black. Black cotton drawstring pants. A black cotton poet shirt. And a black bandanna wrapped around his ponytail.

Lila finished her drink and put the coconut shell in the trash can. "So now what?" she asked Mandy.

"Why do you keep asking me?" Mandy said irritably. "You're the one with the guidebook. Can't *you* suggest something?"

"I suggested shopping," Lila reminded her. "You guys vetoed that idea."

"And I suggested art galleries," Mandy said, her voice breaking. "But you guys didn't want to do that. And even if you did, we couldn't, because every single place we go, we see Jack and Ellen." She rested her head on her forearms.

Lila studied Mandy out of the corner of her eye. She couldn't help noticing that Mandy's voice cracked a little when she said the name *Jack*.

Kimberly sighed and dumped her coconut drink into the trash can. "Maybe we should just go back to the ship. That way, we can each do what we want to do." She leaned down and dipped her fingers into the fountain to wash off the stickiness. "Hey, look! There's money at the bottom. This must be a wishing well."

"You know what I wish," Mandy said angrily. "I wish I'd never come on this stupid cruise."

And with that, she burst into tears and began running down the street toward the dock where the tender picked up the passengers for the ship.

"What's with her?" Kimberly asked. "Was it something I said?"

Lila stared at Mandy, chewing the inside of her lip. Hmmm. Mandy wasn't usually that touchy. Maybe she was getting sick of nonstop Unicorn company too.

Maybe she'd rather be spending some time with a kindred spirit. Like Jack.

"I really had fun today," Ellen told Jack, fumbling in Mandy's wicker bag for the key to her cabin. They had returned to the ship, and Jack had insisted on seeing Ellen to her door.

"Ellen," he said, taking her hand. "I had fun this

morning too. You're a very, very special girl. So creative. So . . . " Several unruly curls had escaped from his bandanna. When he leaned down to kiss her, she felt them brush softly against her cheek and forehead.

It was a nice kiss. Sweet and tender. Ellen's heart fluttered, and she felt butterflies in her stomach.

He lifted his head and his soulful eyes gazed hopefully into hers. "Can we get together tonight? The movie theater is showing a foreign film by Pierre DuChamp. His films are beautiful. Like impressionist paintings."

Ellen hesitated, then said something that she had never in her whole life expected to say. "I'm so sorry, Jack. But I have another date."

Jessica sat with Kimberly and Lila at the Top Side Café. She looked around and couldn't help noticing that by now, many of the passengers seemed to have paired off. Most of the tables were occupied by couples. Some of them were even holding hands.

After the girls had returned to the ship, Mandy had gone to the cabin, disappeared into the bathroom, and emerged twenty minutes later with red and swollen eyes. She'd told Jessica and Kimberly she had a headache and didn't want any lunch. So they'd left her in the cabin to take a nap.

"Think Mandy should go to the infirmary?"

Kimberly asked, chewing her vegetable sandwich.

Lila rolled her eyes. "I don't think she's sick in *that* way."

Jessica lifted her sunglasses so she could look at Lila directly. "Do you think she's sick in some other way?"

Lila set down her drink. "Think about it, you guys. It's killing Mandy to see Ellen with Jack."

Kimberly's eyes widened. "You mean . . ."

"I mean, Mandy's figured out that he's totally perfect for her," Lila said with satisfaction.

Jessica nodded slowly. She never thought of Lila as the most perceptive person in the world, but now she had to give her credit—what she said really did make sense.

Kimberly wiped her mouth with a napkin. "Well, hey, Mandy shouldn't lose hope. I mean, why would Ellen necessarily chose Jack when there's a great guy like Peter around." Suddenly, Kimberly went a little pale. She set down her sandwich, as though she were feeling sick. "Of course, she might not choose Peter either. She's got a date with Sam right now."

Jessica felt a knot in her chest. For some reason, she didn't feel so psyched that Ellen was getting ready to go dolphin spotting with Sam—who happened to be the cutest, funnest guy Jessica had met all year.

"There's one!" Sam handed Ellen the binoculars. "Wow! This is fantastic! It's fabulous! It's like

being right next to him." Ellen couldn't actually see
a thing. It was too hard to get the binoculars aimed
at the right spot.

She and Sam were sitting on *The Dol Fin,* a boat
and restaurant that took passengers out from Claire
Isle to see the dolphins.

Ellen handed Sam back the binoculars and he
put them in the case. Then he picked up his soup
spoon and took a taste. "Wow!" he said.

"Wow is right," Ellen said after taking a sip of
her own soup. It was seafood soup. Ellen didn't
like seafood, so she wasn't a great judge of seafood
soup. She wondered if Sam meant "wow" as in
good or "wow" as in bad.

Sam took another sip. "Whooaaa!"

Ellen took another sip and smiled. "You said it."

"What do you think?" Sam asked.

"What do *you* think?" she hedged.

"I think we're thinking the same thing," he said
with a sly smile.

"I'll bet you're right." Ellen began to sweat
under her visor. *Where* was this conversation
going?

Sam signaled the waiter. "Could we get some
hot sauce?" he asked. "It's good but a little bland."

"Certainly," the waiter replied.

Sam leaned his elbow on the table and rested his
chin in the palm of his hand. "We're really on the
same wavelength, and it is so great. We're both into

people, and music, and seafood, and . . . " He reached across the table and took her hand. "I'm glad Jessica introduced us."

Ellen gazed at Sam's wide smile. He had perfect teeth. Straight. White. Even. He could be in a toothpaste commercial. He was so incredibly good-looking.

Two girls sat at the table next to theirs. They were watching Sam and Ellen, but trying to look like they weren't. Ellen turned her face toward them and gave them the kind of smile other girls usually gave her—friendly, but with just a tinge of sympathy.

It was the kind of smile Lila gave Ellen when Ellen was drooling over something that she could never afford, but Lila could.

It was the kind of smile Kimberly gave her when Kimberly got the blue ribbon for some sport, and Ellen got a pat on the head for a "good try."

It was the kind of smile Jessica gave her when Jessica got the joke, and Ellen didn't.

It was a smile that said, *It must be really hard to be such a big drip, and boy am I glad it's you and not me.*

"I'm glad Jessica introduced us too," Ellen purred. "It's changed my life."

Ten

Lila lay on her bed staring at her red slip dress hanging on the hook on the back of the door so that all the creases could fall out in time for tonight.

The red slip dress that Lila had bought for her dream cruise.

The red slip dress that Ellen was going to wear on her dream date.

Lila reached for a nail file and began to saw thoughtfully at the edge of her already perfectly manicured thumbnail.

It was a gorgeous day. She was on a floating pleasure palace. She was accompanied by her four best friends and a wardrobe that was to die for.

So why was she lying in a cabin by herself, so bored she was filing her own nails? Nobody wanted to do anything. Or at least nobody wanted to do anything that anybody else wanted to do.

Mandy was in her cabin brooding. Jessica had gone off somewhere on her own. That was OK with Lila since she was sort of sick of Jessica.

She could hang out with Kimberly if she wanted to go jog or lift weights or something. But she didn't. She was not into physical exercise. In France, they had machines that exercised your body while you just lay there reading a magazine.

I wish I'd gone to France, she thought glumly.

The door flew open and Ellen came racing in, dressed like Jessica. Short white skirt, striped orange-and-white polyester tank, a white visor, and tennis shoes with orange laces.

She snatched off the visor and kicked off the shoes, diving down into her drawer and pulling out some running shorts. "I've got to hurry. I'm meeting Peter for a jog and then we're going to a lecture. Oh, wow, Lila. What a *superfantastic* day. I had lunch with Sam and we had the most *fabulous* seafood stew. It was soooo delicious . . ."

"Oh, knock it off," Lila snapped. "You hate seafood and you know it."

Ellen raised her eyebrows. "What's the matter with you?"

"Nothing," Lila muttered. "But Sam's not around so you can cut the Ms. Perky act."

"Don't be mad at me because I went out with Sam. I'm going out with Jared tonight. Remember?"

Like I could really forget? Lila stood up. "I'm going to get a manicure," she announced.

"OK," Ellen said in a subdued tone. "Sure. I'll see you later."

Lila left the cabin and headed for the beauty shop. Maybe she'd get her hair conditioned too. And a facial. But then, why bother? It wasn't like *she* was going to dinner at the VIP lounge in a red silk slip dress.

"I believe in pacing myself," Peter said, jogging along at a nice easy pace. They were on the track that circled the perimeter of the top deck. There were three lanes. People jogged in one direction on the outside two lanes, and in the other direction on the inside lane.

Ellen had expected to have a hard time keeping up, but she was having no trouble at all. Peter was a good coach. He'd given her some tips on breathing and stretching, and the run actually felt pretty good.

"Hey!" he said. "Look who's coming."

Ellen saw Kimberly jogging toward them.

"Hi, Kimberly!" Peter said.

Kimberly's face was pink from exercise. And when she saw them, it turned even pinker. She lifted her hand in a wave, passing them.

Ellen waved back. Was it her imagination, or did Kimberly look a little displeased?

Maybe she was annoyed that Ellen was wearing her own shorts and shoes, and not Kimberly's.

Ellen's shorts weren't any kind of fancy athletic brand. She got them from the discount store.

Maybe Kimberly was afraid Ellen's second-rate running shorts and shoes were making a bad impression on Peter. Maybe Kimberly thought Ellen wasn't trying hard enough.

As they started their second lap, Ellen saw Kimberly coming around again.

"What about my form?" Ellen asked. "Is there anything I could do to improve it?"

"Your form is really really good," Peter said as Kimberly jogged past them. "I don't you think you could improve on it."

Ellen smiled. Kimberly couldn't help but overhear that remark.

They continued jogging. She could hear Peter's breathing. It was rhythmic and regular. She tried to synchronize her own breathing. When he inhaled, she inhaled. When he exhaled, she exhaled.

The inside lane was getting more crowded. A group of girls who had been stretching on the medallion stepped onto the inside lane to begin their run. A gorgeous redhead with curls piled high did a double take when she saw Peter, then tripped and fell.

The three girls behind her plowed into her like a three-car pileup on the freeway.

Behind them came Kimberly. She hurried to help the fallen girl and so did Peter.

The redheaded girl blushed and stammered as Peter

helped her to her feet. "Are you all right?" he asked.

"Yes . . . I . . . just . . . ummm . . . thank you for helping me."

"I think I know what your problem is," Peter told her.

The girl's eyes widened and her face turned beet red.

"You're not picking your feet up fast enough. Watch Ellen here, and you'll see how well she moves her feet."

Kimberly made a little strangling noise and began to cough.

"Are you all right?" Peter asked Kimberly.

"Fine," she managed to say.

"I'll bet you didn't drink enough water before you came out here, did you?" Peter waggled his finger at Kimberly. "Take care of your body, and your body will take care of you," he chided her gently. "Come on, Ellen."

He took Ellen's hand and tugged slightly. Ellen broke into a jog and Peter fell into step beside her. She couldn't help smiling. Peter had made it obvious he was really into her.

Kimberly was probably thrilled.

"'Watch Ellen' he said!" Kimberly paced up and down the cabin like a caged tiger. "*Ellen!* Can you believe that?"

Mandy pressed the cold washcloth against her

face. "Would you please quit shouting. My head is killing me. I always get a headache when I cry."

Kimberly had been ranting and raving for over a half an hour and Mandy was tired of it. Kimberly was always the first one to accuse the others of whining, but when somebody threw a spoke in her wheel, she whined the longest and the loudest.

"Quit complaining," Jessica said from inside the bathroom where she was applying fresh makeup. "You're the one who thought Peter was perfect for Ellen. You're the one who *insisted* that she go out with him. Why are you complaining now?"

Kimberly leaned over on the dresser and groaned. "Because it didn't hit me until about the third lap. *I* was jogging by myself. Alone. Not even a girlfriend to keep me company. While *Ellen* is skipping around the track with the most incredible hunk on the ship. And *I* introduced them." She lifted her head and smacked her palm against her forehead three times while she chanted, "Dumb . . . dumb . . . dumb."

Jack lifted Ellen high over his head. She arched her back and threw back her arms in a graceful curve. A long, chiffon scarf floated out behind them as he ran, bearing her incredibly graceful form like a feather.

He lowered her gently, then tossed her into the air, as if she were a bird. She flew, turning round and round surrounded by a rainbow of graceful scarves, landing on the points of her toes.

The audience gasped and applauded.

Ellen looked out and saw Mandy, Kimberly, Lila, and Jessica sitting in the front row. They blew kisses.

A rose landed suddenly at her feet. She looked to see who had thrown it. Jared came leaping out of the wings onto the stage. She ran—but not too fast. Just as she had hoped, he caught her, and they began to dance an elegant waltz. As they waltzed past a tree, a foot came protruding out from behind it. Jared tripped. And Peter and Sam jumped out. They each grabbed an arm. Tugging her this way and that.

The music of steel drums grew louder and more discordant. "Help! Help!" she cried.

Suddenly, a wave came rolling toward the stage from the back of the theater. Curtis came riding toward her on a big white surfboard. The wave broke over the stage, pulling Sam, Ellen, and Peter apart.

Ellen flailed about, her chiffon scarf tangling around her arms and legs. She tried to cry out for help, but it was no use. Her mouth was full of water. She was going under when suddenly, Curtis reached down and pulled her up beside him on the surfboard.

Gasping, she held on to his waist and they stood poised on the board until the water began to subside.

The orchestra pit was full of water, but the musicians played as they sat in floating deck chairs. The music built to a romantic crescendo. Curtis took her in his arms for the final moment of the ballet. She lifted her face to his, but before they could kiss . . .

Splat!

"*Eww!*" *Curtis groaned. Something soft and squashy had just hit him on the shoulder. It looked like a rotten tomato.*

Ellen heard several boos and jeers from the audience. She looked out to see who could have been so mean and so rude as to throw rotten fruit and saw Jessica winding up like a pitcher with a mango in her hand.

She ducked, but not fast enough.

Splat!

The smelly fruit landed right on Ellen's skirt.

She heard roars of laughter from the audience.

"You think that's so funny, Jessica?" Ellen yelled, starting to get furious. "Guess what? This is your *skirt!" She threw back her head and began to laugh. "Ha ha ha ha ha ha ha!"*

Curtis shook her arm. "Ellen!"

"Ha ha ha ha ha ha!" she roared.

"Ellen! Ellen!" Curtis shook her arm even harder.

Ellen's eyes flew open.

"Ellen!" Peter was hissing. "Wake up." She realized it was Peter shaking her arm. She blinked, looking around. Where was she?

She saw Captain Jackson standing on a small stage looking straight at her.

Oh, no! They were in the small auditorium and she had fallen asleep during Captain Jackson's lecture.

"Was I snoring?" she whispered out of the side of her mouth, sitting up straight.

"No," he whispered back. "You were laughing. Sort of."

There weren't many people at the lecture. Maybe fifteen. And they looked like total study hounds. Everybody in the room except Ellen and Peter seemed to be taking notes. Ellen guessed they were going to write some kind of report—for fun.

Well. It took all kinds.

"Any more questions?" Captain Jackson asked.

No one raised their hand.

"Then I thank you all for your attention and hope you enjoyed my lecture and slide show."

The fifteen people in the audience applauded politely and stood.

"Want to go talk to Captain Jackson?" Peter asked. "So you can tell your friends you've spoken to him personally."

"No thanks," Ellen said. "I've already had the pleasure."

A pleasure that would be repeated tonight in the VIP dining room.

Ellen yawned. She was glad she'd had a chance to take a nap. Otherwise, she would have been dead on her feet tonight. She wasn't sure she was cut out to be a social butterfly. It was exhausting.

Eleven

Lila knocked on the door.

"Come in," Mandy called out.

Lila opened the door. Mandy, Kimberly, and Jessica all lay on their beds. Crumpled, used tissues were everywhere. The room was wall-to-wall red swollen eyes and red swollen noses. Lila lifted her lip in a sneer. "You guys are pathetic."

"Hey! We've got enough problems without taking a bunch of abuse from you. Why don't you go back to your own cabin?" Kimberly grabbed another tissue and angrily blew her nose.

Lila sat down in the one little armchair and looked at her newly polished nails. "Because I don't feel like watching Cinderella dress for the ball."

"And you call *us* pathetic." Jessica reached for her soda and took a sip. "You can't stand to see

Ellen get all dressed up to go out with your guy."

"Wrong," Lila said. She ran her fingers through her silky hair. "You know, there's nothing like a hot oil treatment, a mud wrap, and a manicure and a pedicure to put things in perspective. I was sitting there feeling really sorry for myself because Ellen was going out tonight and I wasn't. And then it hit me. I, Lila Fowler, am actually worried about competing with Ellen Riteman."

"Strange but true," Kimberly mumbled.

"But we're not," Lila said. "Don't you see? We're not competing with Ellen. We're competing with *ourselves.*"

"Huh?" Jessica asked.

"Ellen can't keep up the act forever," Lila began. "And even if she could, she's not going to keep them all. It's only a ten-day cruise. She doesn't have time."

Jessica sat up. "So what are you saying?"

"I'm saying that by tomorrow, Ellen will have had four dates. She'll decide which guy she wants, and then cut the other three loose. So why should we all be miserable, when only one of us is going to turn out to be a big-time loser?"

Mandy brushed her hair back off her forehead. "Yeah. But which one of us?"

Lila sat back, lowered her eyelids, and felt very much a woman of the world. It wasn't going to be her—that was for sure. Not after she'd sawed almost all the way through the high thin heels that went with that red slip dress. Not after she'd reminded Ellen that she was supposed to think table manners were only for lesser social beings. And not after she'd advised her to tic out at least once every ten minutes.

"Lila's right," Jessica said. "And you know what I think we should do? I think we should get all dolled up, go to the disco, and meet some guys. That's what we came for. What are we doing sitting around here?"

Kimberly jumped up and raced into the bathroom. "I get the sink first," she shouted happily.

"Ms. Riteman, how nice to see you again." Captain Jackson sounded less than sincere. Ellen couldn't exactly blame him for his lack of enthusiasm. They hadn't exactly met under the most auspicious of circumstances the first time. And the second time she had fallen asleep during his lecture and slide show.

"Nice to see you," she answered, trying to keep her voice from quavering.

Even though she was wearing Lila's red silk dress (which probably cost more than Ellen's house) and Lila's matching red silk high heels, she didn't feel like a rich eccentric. She felt like she was about to eat dinner in the principal's office.

Ellen and Jared were the first people to arrive in the captain's private dining room. It was absolutely the most elegant room Ellen had ever seen.

The large round table, set for ten, was covered

with a snowy white cloth. In the center, a huge silver urn held an arrangement of tall tropical flowers in red, pink, and orange. The walls were a dark, paneled wood, heavily varnished and ornamented with shiny brass sconces.

She didn't care what Lila had said, no way would she have the nerve to eat with her fingers.

Her left eyebrow began to twitch nervously—all by itself.

More guests began to arrive and Jared and Lila were introduced to the governor of Claire Isle and his wife; the ship's physician, Dr. Woodard Kenny; Danny Orisman, the son of the famous movie director; Tommy and Anna Beardsley, the twin son and daughter of Thomas Beardsley as in Beardsley, Beardsley, Beardsley, and Beardsley (makers of fine cutlery since 1824 and now a wholly owned subsidiary of Beardsley Amalgamated Chemical & Steel); and last but not least, Kickie Crookshank, the youngest U.S. gold medalist for diving.

"Wow!" Jared whispered. "This is some get-together."

Tommy and Anna introduced themselves to Jared and Ellen while a white-coated steward carried cups of punch on a silver tray.

Ellen took one and decided to postpone her tic attack. A: She didn't want to slop punch all over somebody with a lot of background in cutlery. And B: She just didn't have the nerve to act like a fool surrounded by all these important people.

Tommy and Anna began to talk to Jared about somebody they all knew, and Captain Jackson came over and smiled down at Ellen. "You appear to have made friends, Ms. Riteman. Is it safe to assume you will be staying for the duration of the cruise?"

"I think so," Ellen replied. "I'm sorry if I seemed rude this afternoon when I fell asleep. I hope you won't hold it against my friend, Peter. It's just that . . ."

Captain Jackson smiled and held up his hand. "Don't worry. And if it's any consolation, your companion slept during most of my lecture too."

"Really?"

Captain Jackson nodded and winked. "Really."

Ellen's eyebrow quit twitching, and she took a sip of her punch. Her stomach began to settle down and she looked around. Now that she wasn't so nervous, she was starting to enjoy being all dressed up and rubbing shoulders with the crème de la crème.

I could get used to this, she thought happily.

"How does my lipstick look?" Jessica shouted.

"Fine?" Mandy shouted back. "What about mine?"

Jessica nodded. "Great."

They stood along the sidelines of the dance floor watching the dancers. They'd been standing there an awfully long time, Jessica thought. Fifteen minutes at least. And so far, nobody had shown any signs at all of asking them to dance.

Kimberly folded her arms. Jessica pinched her. "Don't do that," she whispered in Kimberly's ear. "It makes you look like a wallflower."

Kimberly nodded and put her hands on her hips.

"Don't do that either," Jessica said. "It makes you look like a security guard."

A look of annoyance spread across Kimberly's face. "Save the advice for Ellen, OK?" Then she turned and disappeared into the crowd.

Jessica turned to Mandy and shrugged. Sometimes Kimberly was just so impossible. She lost her cool so easily. Sure, it was tough standing around a disco, all glammed out and not being asked to dance. But getting asked to dance was an art. And a science. You had to take it step by step. And do it just right.

Step one was you had to look like you were having a great time. She smiled and moved her head and shoulders to create the *impression of dancing*, even though she wasn't really dancing. Body language was key. She looked like she wanted to dance. And she didn't look like a wallflower. Or somebody afraid to be noticed.

Step two was getting noticed. It was best to give a good twenty seconds. She counted to twenty, keeping her eyes on the dance floor, smiling and moving to the beat.

When she hit twenty, she moved onto step three: eye contact.

Jessica began looking around the room, trying to find somebody who had been watching her. She could usually find at least three or four guys. Then, as soon as she locked on, she turned up the wattage on the smile, and . . . presto . . . the guy came trotting over.

She looked around the room. Nobody was looking at her.

She looked around again. She must have missed something.

She looked around yet another time.

A couple of guys were looking around the room too. But their eyes flickered past her, obviously searching for someone else.

A finger tapped her on the shoulder. Aha! She turned. A tall, good-looking guy with close-cropped hair gave her a shy smile. "Excuse me," he said. "But aren't you a friend of that girl, Ellen?"

"Yes," Jessica answered.

"Is she here tonight?" the guy asked.

"No."

"Bummer," the guy said. He smiled. "Thanks anyway. I was just kind of hoping I might get to talk to her. I've seen her around and . . . well . . . I was hoping I could get to meet her." He backed away. "Have fun."

Jessica felt her lower jaw go slack. This wasn't happening. It couldn't be happening. She had stepped into some kind of parallel universe and . . .

"Who was that?" Mandy asked.

"Some guy who wanted to meet Ellen!"

"Everybody wants to meet Ellen," Mandy said. "Everybody's seen her out with the four cutest guys on board, and they think she's got to be a movie star or something."

Jessica groaned. "I can't stand any more of this. Come on. Let's round up the others and get out of here."

The captain's steward held up a tiny triangle and tapped it, producing a silvery, bell tone. "Dinner is served."

The group moved toward the dinner table where white place cards instructed guests on where to sit.

Jared was seated next to Anna Beardsley.

And Ellen was seated next to the governor of Claire Isle.

Ellen reached for the back of her chair, but the governor beat her to it and politely pulled it back for her. "Oh, thank you, your excellency," Ellen said in her most cultivated voice.

"My pleasure," he replied.

Ellen started to step around when suddenly, the ground beneath her swayed. "Oh dear!" she yipped.

Everyone turned their heads.

The ground became so unsteady, Ellen could hardly stand. "Whoooaaaaa!" she cried, windmilling her arms for balance.

"Ellen?" Jared started toward her.

But it was too late. Ellen suddenly collapsed, falling forward into the table. The table tipped and the plates, glasses, silverware, and centerpiece went crashing to the floor.

"Ellen! Ellen!"

The doctor was at her side immediately.

"Lie still," he ordered. "Don't move. Call the infirmary and tell them to get a gurney up here, stat," he barked at the steward. He gently took Ellen's hand and began to check her pulse. "Ellen! Ellen! Can you hear me?"

Ellen could hear him just fine. But she was so embarrassed, she just couldn't bring herself to open her eyes. It was just easier to pretend she was out cold.

What had she done? she wondered as she felt herself being lifted onto a gurney. Tripped over her own feet?

"This Ellen thing will be over by tomorrow morning," Lila said. "I promise. And I think we made a big tactical error leaving the disco like that. We should have stayed until you guys met somebody new."

The Unicorns were gathered in Lila's cabin with a couple of bags of popcorn, two bags of miniature chocolate bars, and two six packs of sodas.

"Us guys," Jessica repeated. "How do you figure *us* guys need to meet somebody new and *you* don't? Ellen could pick Jared, and then you'd be the dateless wonder."

Lila chuckled. "I don't think that's going to happen."

"How come?" Kimberly shoved a mouthful of popcorn into her mouth.

"There's a reason my dad is one of the richest men in the country," Lila replied with satisfaction. "He knows how to look after his interests. I'm his daughter. And I know a thing or two about looking after my interests too."

"What are you talking about?" Mandy asked.

"I'm one hundred percent sure that Ellen's going to make a complete fool out of herself tonight, and Jared is probably never going to want to see her again."

"In other words, you fixed her little red wagon?" Kimberly snickered.

"Nope. Her little red shoes. *My* little red shoes. She ought to be falling off them right about now. And with any luck, she'll fall right in the captain's lap."

Jessica's eyes widened. "I can't believe you—"

There was a knock on the door, and Lila jumped up to answer it. "Jared!"

Jared stood in the doorway, looking serious. "I thought I'd better come and tell you. Ellen is fine. She's just fine. But she's in the infirmary. She fainted."

"Fainted?" Lila repeated.

"The doctor says she's going to be fine. He can't find anything wrong. So it must be exhaustion. He wants her to spend the night there."

"Should we go see her?" Lila asked.

Jared shook his head. "No. The doctor said she should probably have complete quiet. But you can see her in the morning." He smiled sadly. "She's a wonderful girl. So . . . fragile. Like fine porcelain. I'll see you tomorrow," he said softly. "Good night."

Lila closed the door and turned, feeling like somebody who'd been hit over the head. "I don't believe this."

"The doctor said she'd be OK," Mandy said. "Let's not get too worried. Ellen's done more in one day than she usually does in a month. No wonder she fainted."

"Doesn't look to me like Jared's losing interest." Jessica picked up the bag of popcorn and plopped down in the middle of Lila's bed.

"No." Lila frowned. "It doesn't."

Mandy sat down and rested her chin in her hand. "We're all in the same boat now. Pun intended."

Nobody laughed.

Twelve

"Here's another one!" the nurse chirped. "My goodness, what a popular girl!"

Ellen took the last bite of her breakfast and admired the four flower arrangements lined up on the enamel table at the foot of her bed.

She still wasn't sure what had happened last night. But her fainting act had been pretty convincing, and now, according to the doctor, she was exhausted.

That was fine with her. She could use a few hours of rest.

The nurse handed her the card that had come with the fourth arrangement and bustled off.

Ellen had received flowers from Jared, Sam, and Jack. "Feel better soon! Peter!" said the fourth card.

She was pleased, but a little disappointed too. She wondered if Curtis knew she was in the infirmary.

He had been the first and only person to bring her flowers the last time she'd wound up here.

The nurse came bustling back. "Your friends are here!"

Ellen tucked the card back in the envelope and felt her heart swell as Mandy, Kimberly, Jessica, and Lila came around the curtain partition.

"Hi," Mandy said quietly.

"Hi," Ellen said.

"How do you feel?" Jessica asked.

"I feel fine," Ellen answered. "Tired, but fine." No way was she going to let her friends know she had fallen. Better they should think she fainted from exhaustion. They'd be so embarrassed for her if they knew she'd just been a klutz.

"We feel really guilty," Mandy said.

"You do?" Ellen shrugged. "What do you feel guilty about?"

"We forced you to do too much," Mandy said gently. "We pushed you. Sightseeing with Jack. Dolphin spotting with Sam. Jogging with Peter. Dinner with Jared. It was so unfair of us. And we're sorry."

"You don't have to keep going out with all of them," Jessica added. "Life is short. It's nuts to spend time with a guy you don't really like. I can see why Sam wouldn't be your cup of tea. You have such completely different personalities."

"And Peter is always going to want to go jogging or play tennis or something like that."

Kimberly sat down in the straight chair beside Ellen's bed. "I made you feel like you had to go. What am I? A gym teacher? You're hear to have fun. Not fulfill a PE credit. Forget Peter."

"I was just as bad about Jack." Mandy hung her head. "If you don't want to see him again. It won't hurt my feelings."

"And don't feel like you have to keep seeing Jared for my sake." Lila laughed weakly. "I *threw* him at you. Forced you to be something you're not. Can you forgive me?"

"Can you forgive all of us?" Mandy pleaded.

Ellen felt so guilty she could hardly look Mandy in the eye. They had given her four fabulous guys. Four fabulous dates. The most unforgettable day of her whole life—and she'd actually let herself start thinking about Curtis.

Ellen Riteman, she scolded herself, *you had better start trying to be as good a friend to Mandy, Kimberly, Lila, and Jessica as they've been to you.*

"There's nothing to forgive," Ellen insisted. She was so touched when she thought about how generous her friends had been, her eyes filled with tears. They had lent her clothes. They had taught her how to walk and talk and carry on conversations. They had pushed her to be more than just plain old Ellen Riteman.

They had given her the most precious gift in the whole world.

Popularity.

She wasn't going to let them down now. No way.

"So Ellen," Mandy said softly. "Would you like us to break it to the guys?"

"Yeah, Ellen. Which guys do you want us to break it to?" Kimberly's face was white.

"We can break it to all of them if that's what you want," Jessica assured her.

All of their faces looked tense, tight, grim. And Ellen knew why.

They were expecting her to cave. To fall down on the job. To let them down—the way she always had in the past.

But she wasn't going to do it. Ellen laughed lightly. "What are you talking about? I'm having the time of my life. Four wonderful guys! I'd be an idiot to let any of them go."

She opened her arms and drew her friends toward her in a big group hug. "You guys are the best bunch of friends in the whole world. You tell Jared, Peter, Jack, and Sam I'll be out of here and ready for action by lunchtime. Then you guys just go on and do what you want. You were absolutely right. We're here to meet guys, not clutch at one another's apron strings. Right?"

Ellen has four boyfriends. Find out how she manages them all in THE UNICORN CLUB #17, **Boyfriends for Everyone.**

SIGN UP FOR THE SWEET VALLEY HIGH® FAN CLUB!

Hey, girls! Get all the gossip on Sweet Valley High's® most popular teenagers when you join our fantastic Fan Club! As a member, you'll get all of this really cool stuff:

- Membership Card with your own personal Fan Club ID number
- A Sweet Valley High® Secret Treasure Box
- Sweet Valley High® Stationery
- Official Fan Club Pencil (for secret note writing!)
- Three Bookmarks
- A "Members Only" Door Hanger
- Two Skeins of J. & P. Coats® Embroidery Floss with flower barrette instruction leaflet
- Two editions of *The Oracle* newsletter
- Plus exclusive Sweet Valley High® product offers, special savings, contests, and much more!